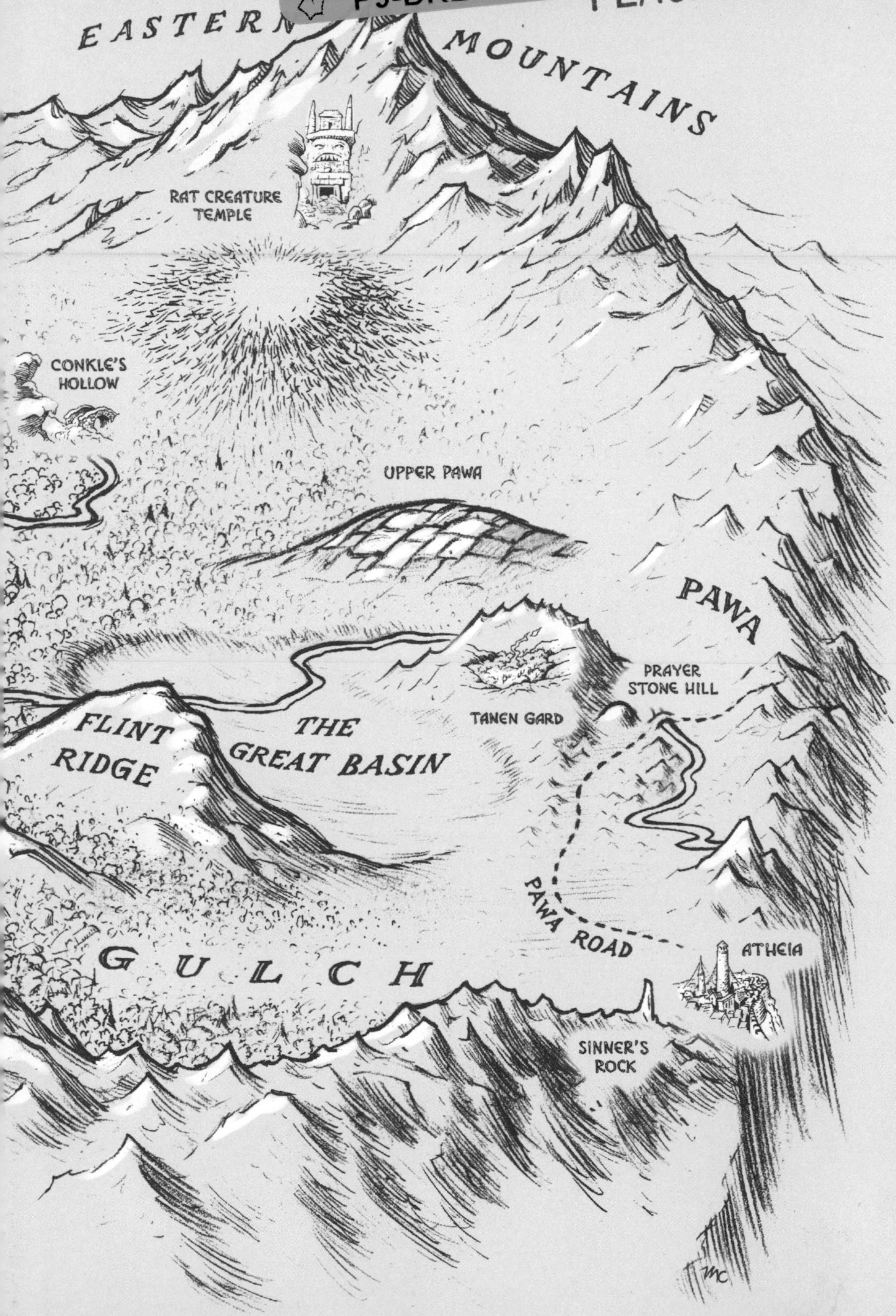
EASTERN
MOUNTAINS
RAT CREATURE TEMPLE
CONKLE'S HOLLOW
UPPER PAWA
PAWA
PRAYER STONE HILL
TANEN GARD
FLINT RIDGE
THE GREAT BASIN
PAWA ROAD
ATHEIA
GULCH
SINNER'S ROCK

Dreaming of Harvestar

ACCLAIM FOR JEFF SMITH'S

Named an all-time top ten graphic novel by **Time** magazine.

"As sweeping as the 'Lord of the Rings' cycle, but much funnier."   —Andrew Arnold, **Time.com**

★"This is first-class kid lit: exciting, funny, scary, and resonant enough that it will stick with readers for a long time."   —**Publishers Weekly**, *starred review*

"One of the best kids' comics ever."   —Vibe *magazine*

"**BONE** is storytelling at its best, full of endearing, flawed characters whose adventures run the gamut from hilarious whimsy . . . to thrilling drama."
                            —**Entertainment Weekly**

"[This] sprawling, mythic comic is spectacular."
                            —**SPIN** *magazine*

"Jeff Smith's cartoons are irresistible. Every gorgeous sweep of his brush speaks volumes."
                            —*Frank Miller, creator of* **Sin City**

OTHER **BONE** BOOKS

Out from Boneville

The Great Cow Race

Eyes of the Storm

The Dragonslayer

Rock Jaw: Master of the Eastern Border

OLD MAN'S CAVE

BY JEFF SMITH

WITH COLOR BY STEVE HAMAKER

An Imprint of

SCHOLASTIC

New York Toronto London Auckland Sydney Mexico City New Delhi Hong Kong Buenos Aires

Library of Congress Catalog Card Number 9568403.
ISBN-13 978-0-439-70628-5 — ISBN-10 0-439-70628-9 (hardcover)
ISBN 0-439-70635-1 (paperback)

ACKNOWLEDGMENTS
Harvestar Family Crest designed by Charles Vess
Map of *The Valley* by Mark Crilley
Color by Steve Hamaker

10 9 8 7 6 5 4   08 09 10
First Scholastic edition, August 2007
Book design by David Saylor
Printed in Singapore 46

This book is for Jim Kammerud

CONTENTS

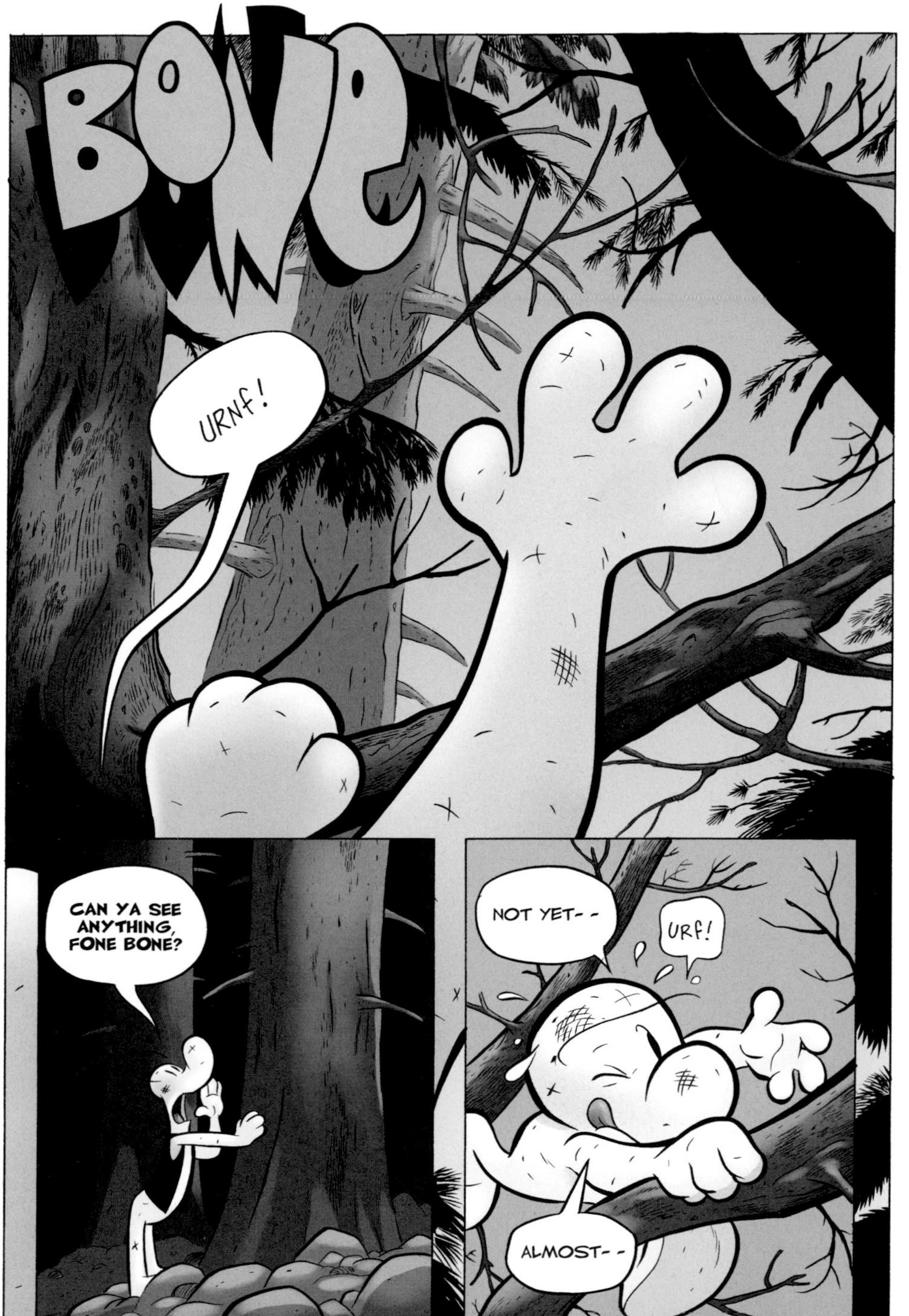
BONE
URNF!
CAN YA SEE ANYTHING, FONE BONE?
NOT YET- -
URF!
ALMOST- -

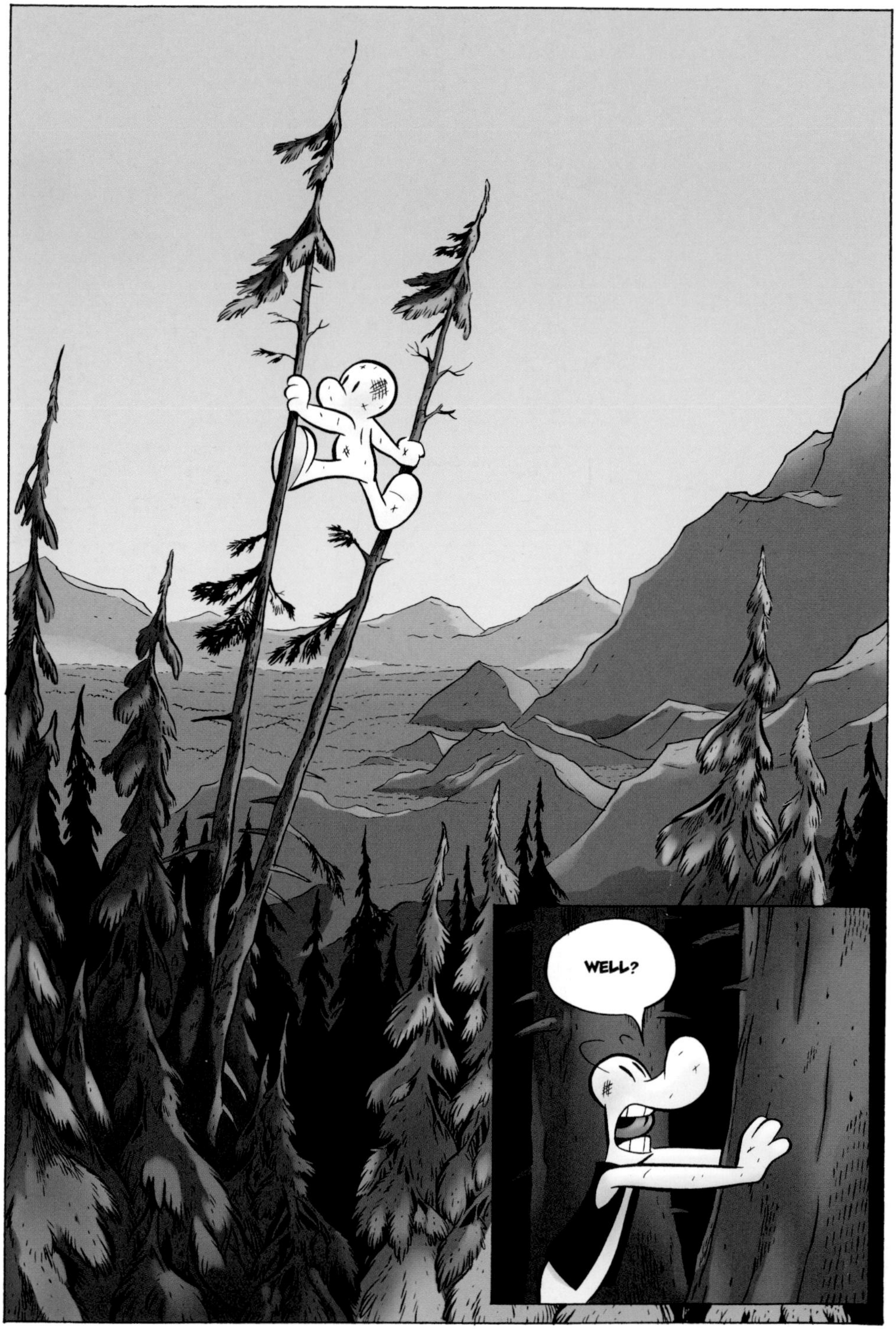
WELL?

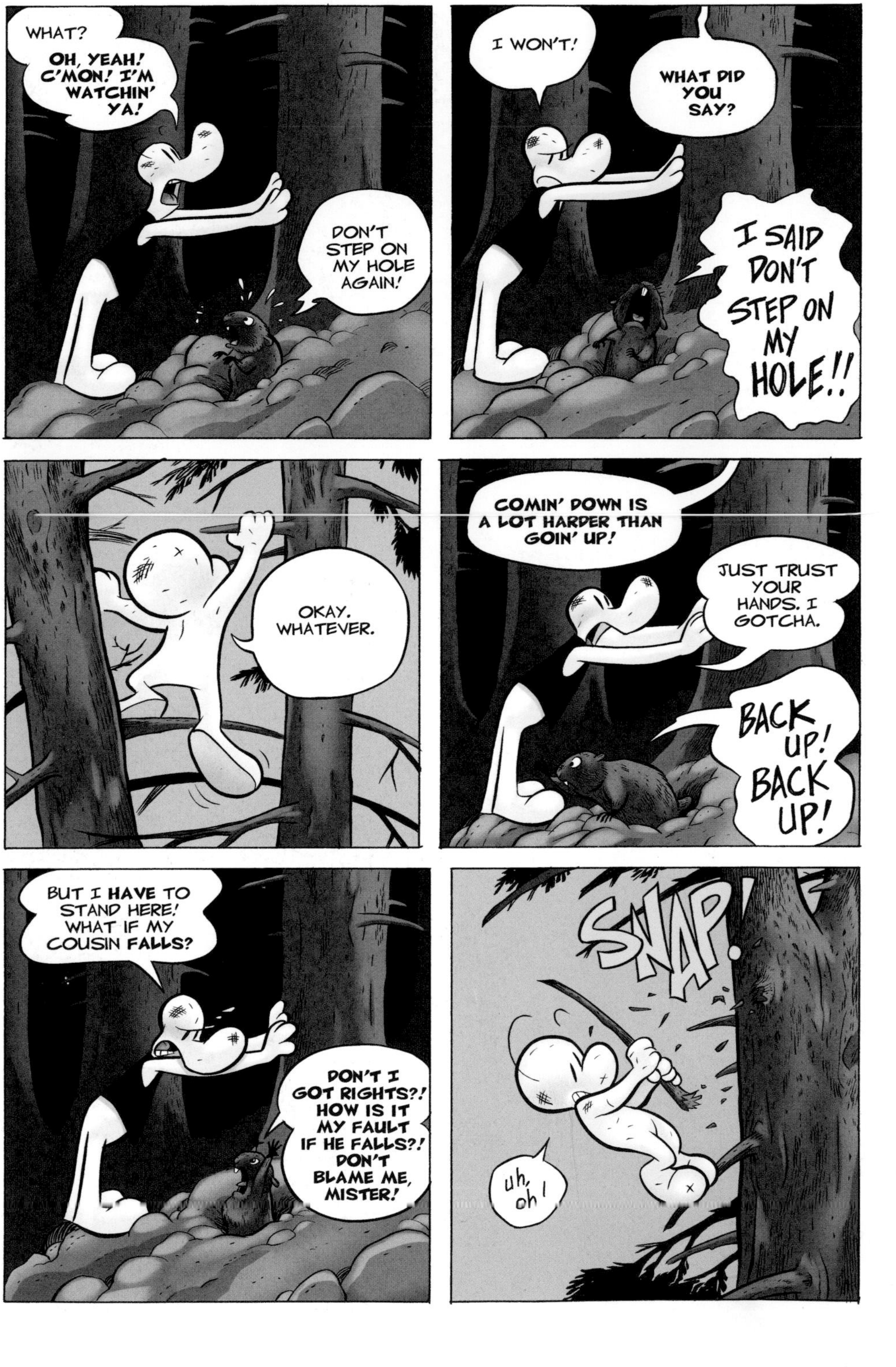
WHAT?
OH, YEAH! C'MON! I'M WATCHIN' YA!
DON'T STEP ON MY HOLE AGAIN!
I WON'T!
WHAT DID YOU SAY?
I SAID DON'T STEP ON MY HOLE!!
OKAY. WHATEVER.
COMIN' DOWN IS A LOT HARDER THAN GOIN' UP!
JUST TRUST YOUR HANDS. I GOTCHA.
BACK UP! BACK UP!
BUT I HAVE TO STAND HERE! WHAT IF MY COUSIN FALLS?
DON'T I GOT RIGHTS?! HOW IS IT MY FAULT IF HE FALLS?! DON'T BLAME ME, MISTER!
SNAP!
uh, oh!

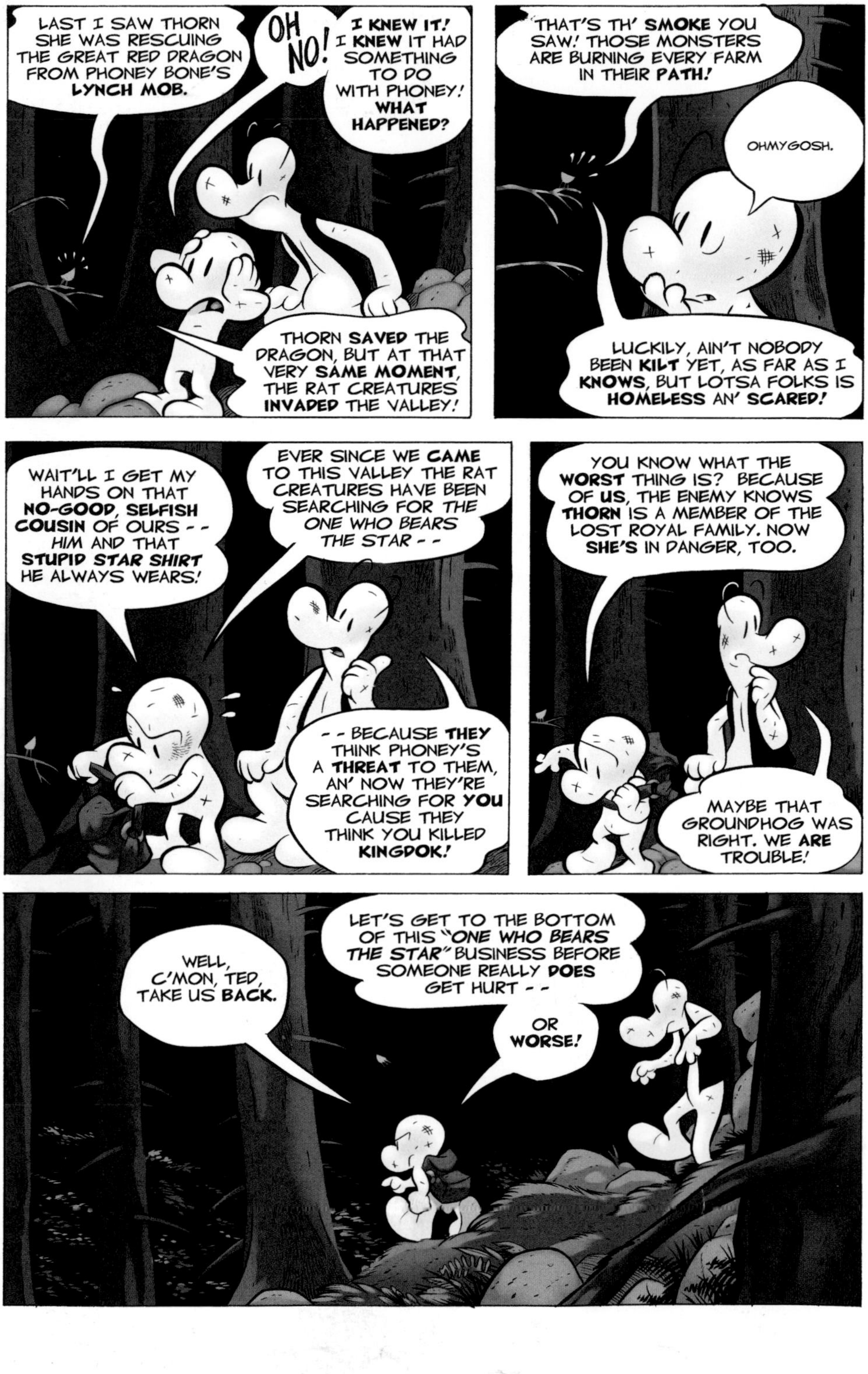
LAST I SAW THORN SHE WAS RESCUING THE GREAT RED DRAGON FROM PHONEY BONE'S **LYNCH MOB.**
OH NO!
I KNEW IT! I **KNEW** IT HAD SOMETHING TO DO WITH PHONEY! **WHAT HAPPENED?**
THORN **SAVED** THE DRAGON, BUT AT THAT VERY **SAME MOMENT**, THE RAT CREATURES **INVADED** THE VALLEY!
THAT'S TH' **SMOKE** YOU SAW! THOSE MONSTERS ARE BURNING EVERY FARM IN THEIR **PATH!**
OHMYGOSH.
LUCKILY, AIN'T NOBODY BEEN **KILT** YET, AS FAR AS I **KNOWS**, BUT LOTSA FOLKS IS **HOMELESS** AN' **SCARED!**
WAIT'LL I GET MY HANDS ON THAT **NO-GOOD, SELFISH COUSIN** OF OURS -- HIM AND THAT **STUPID STAR SHIRT** HE ALWAYS WEARS!
EVER SINCE WE **CAME** TO THIS VALLEY THE RAT CREATURES HAVE BEEN SEARCHING FOR *THE ONE WHO BEARS THE STAR* --
-- BECAUSE **THEY** THINK PHONEY'S A **THREAT** TO THEM, AN' NOW THEY'RE SEARCHING FOR **YOU** CAUSE THEY THINK YOU KILLED **KINGDOK!**
YOU KNOW WHAT THE **WORST** THING IS? BECAUSE OF **US**, THE ENEMY KNOWS **THORN** IS A MEMBER OF THE LOST ROYAL FAMILY. NOW **SHE'S** IN DANGER, TOO.
MAYBE THAT GROUNDHOG WAS RIGHT. WE **ARE** TROUBLE!
WELL, C'MON, TED, TAKE US **BACK.**
LET'S GET TO THE BOTTOM OF THIS "***ONE WHO BEARS THE STAR***" BUSINESS BEFORE SOMEONE REALLY **DOES** GET HURT --
OR **WORSE!**

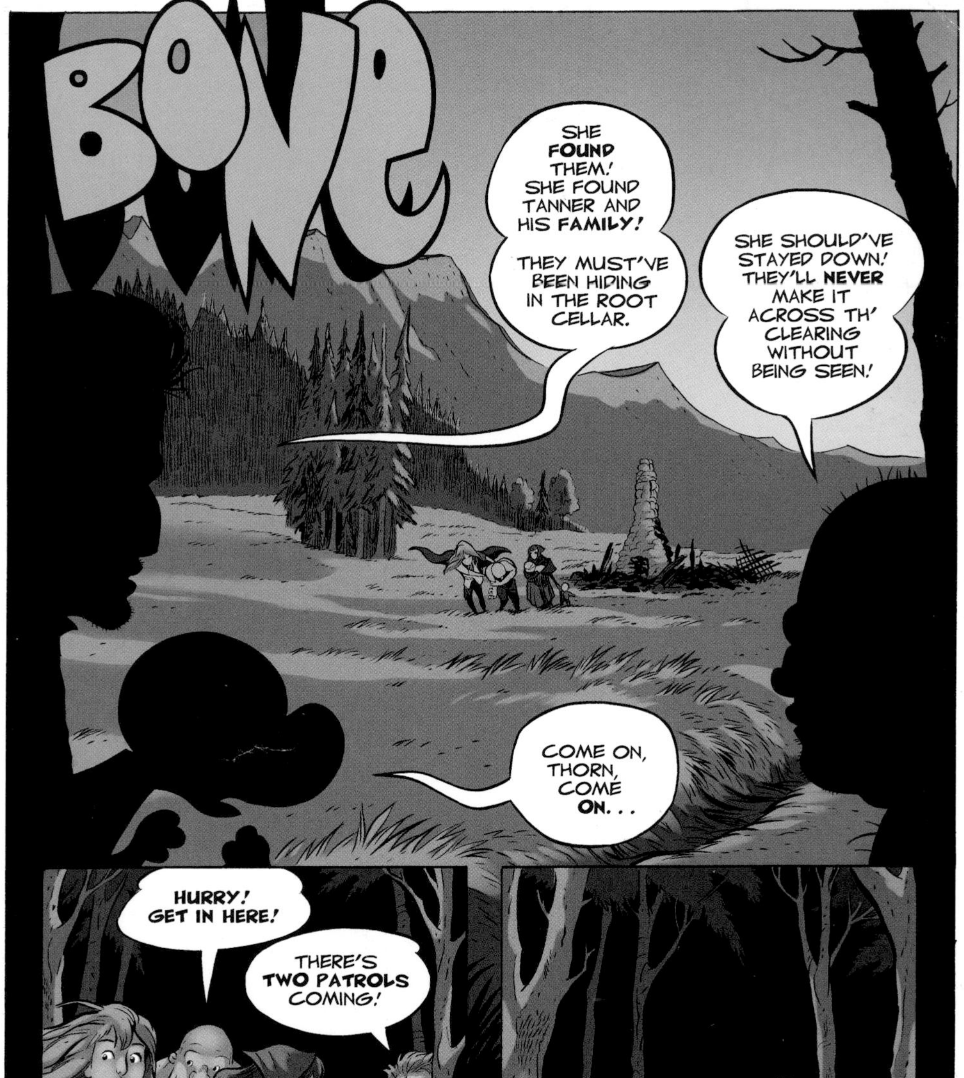
BONE
SHE FOUND THEM! SHE FOUND TANNER AND HIS FAMILY!
THEY MUST'VE BEEN HIDING IN THE ROOT CELLAR.
SHE SHOULD'VE STAYED DOWN! THEY'LL NEVER MAKE IT ACROSS TH' CLEARING WITHOUT BEING SEEN!
COME ON, THORN, COME ON. . .
HURRY! GET IN HERE!
THERE'S TWO PATROLS COMING!

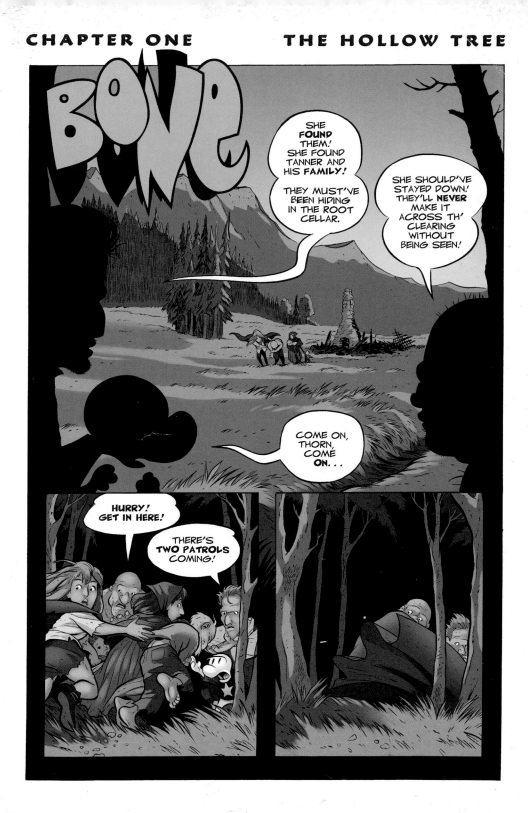

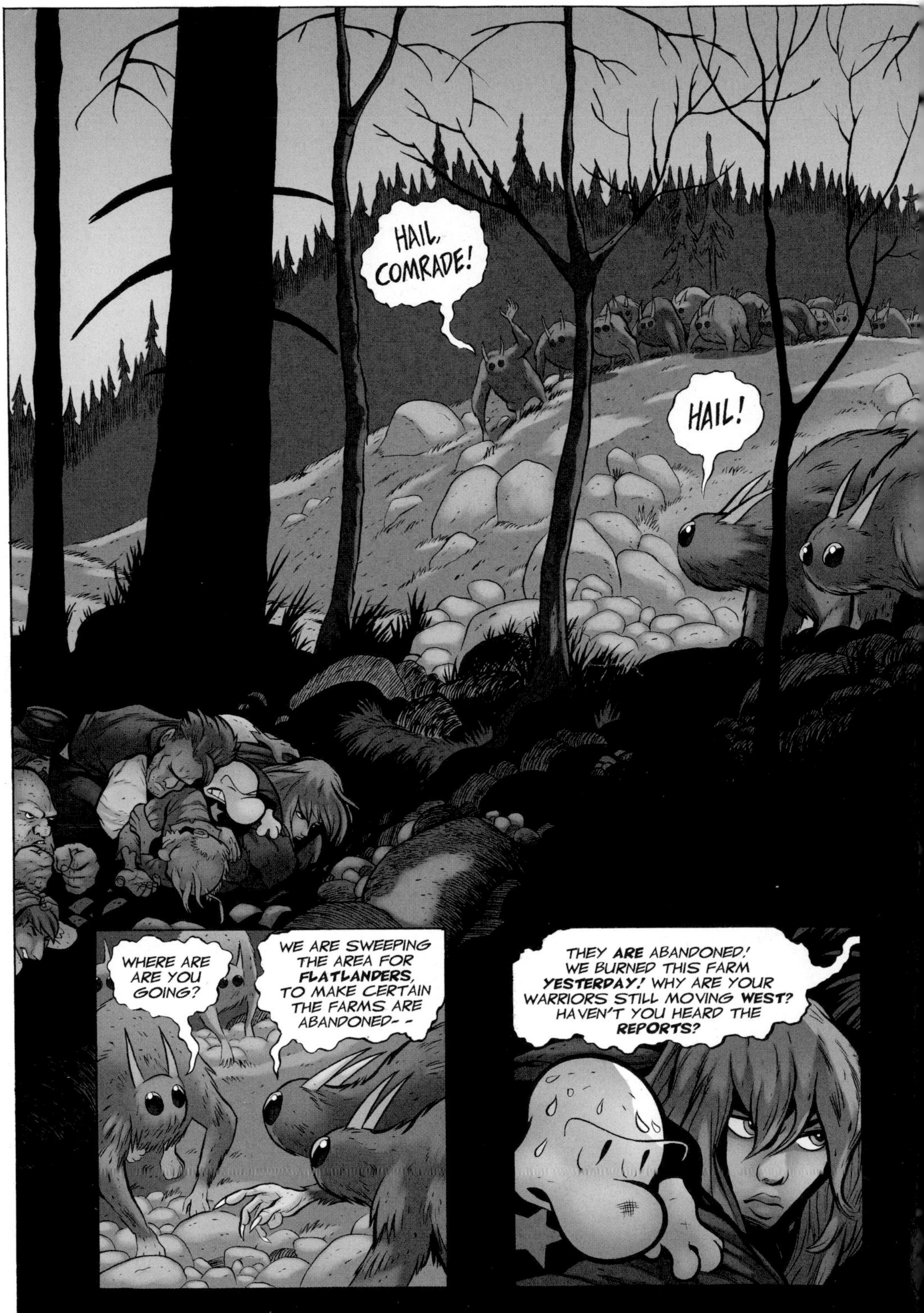
HAIL, COMRADE!
HAIL!
WHERE ARE ARE YOU GOING?
WE ARE SWEEPING THE AREA FOR FLATLANDERS, TO MAKE CERTAIN THE FARMS ARE ABANDONED- -
THEY ARE ABANDONED! WE BURNED THIS FARM YESTERDAY! WHY ARE YOUR WARRIORS STILL MOVING WEST? HAVEN'T YOU HEARD THE REPORTS?

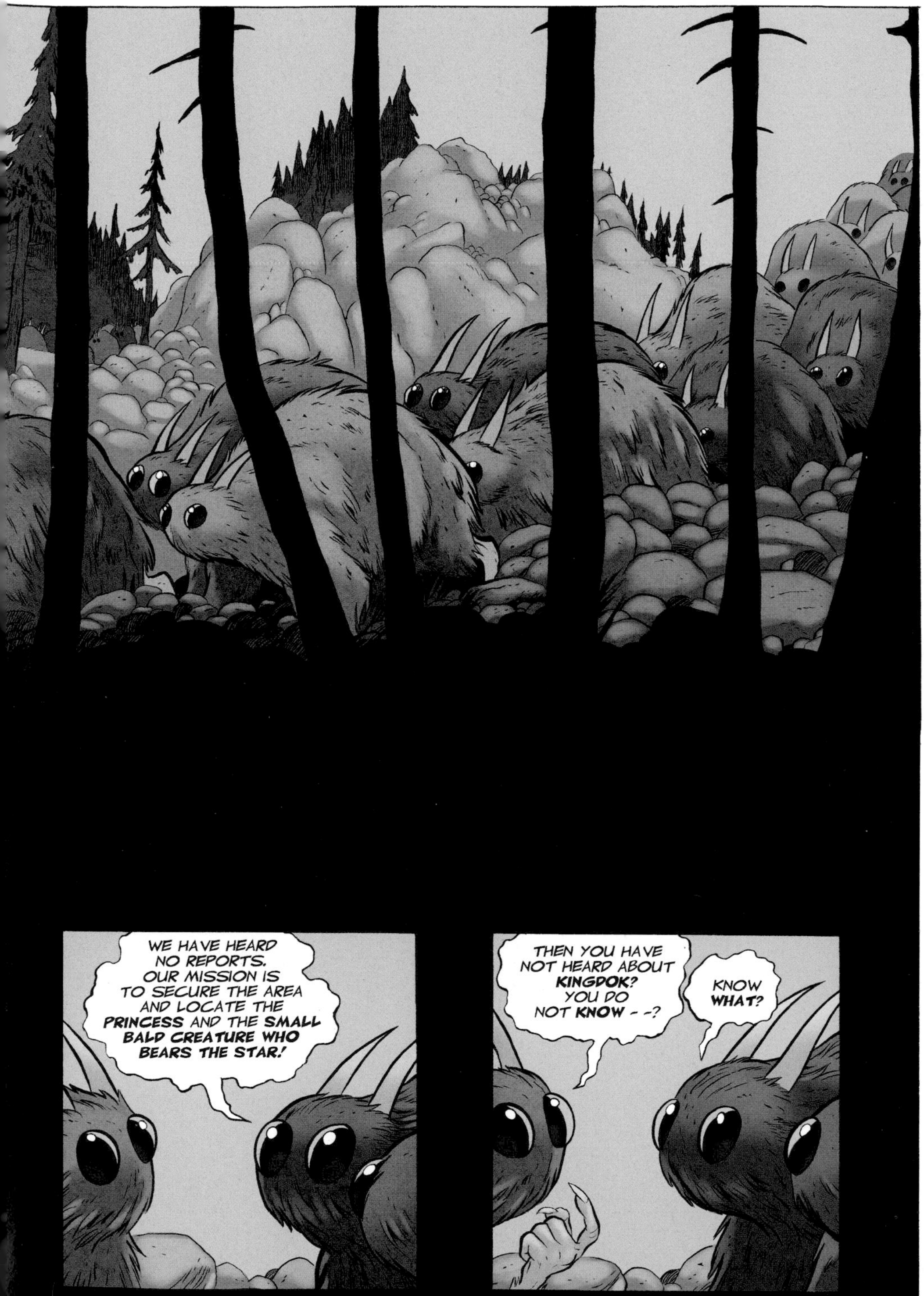
WE HAVE HEARD NO REPORTS. OUR MISSION IS TO SECURE THE AREA AND LOCATE THE **PRINCESS** AND THE **SMALL BALD CREATURE WHO BEARS THE STAR!**
THEN YOU HAVE NOT HEARD ABOUT **KINGDOK?** YOU DO NOT **KNOW** - -?
KNOW **WHAT?**

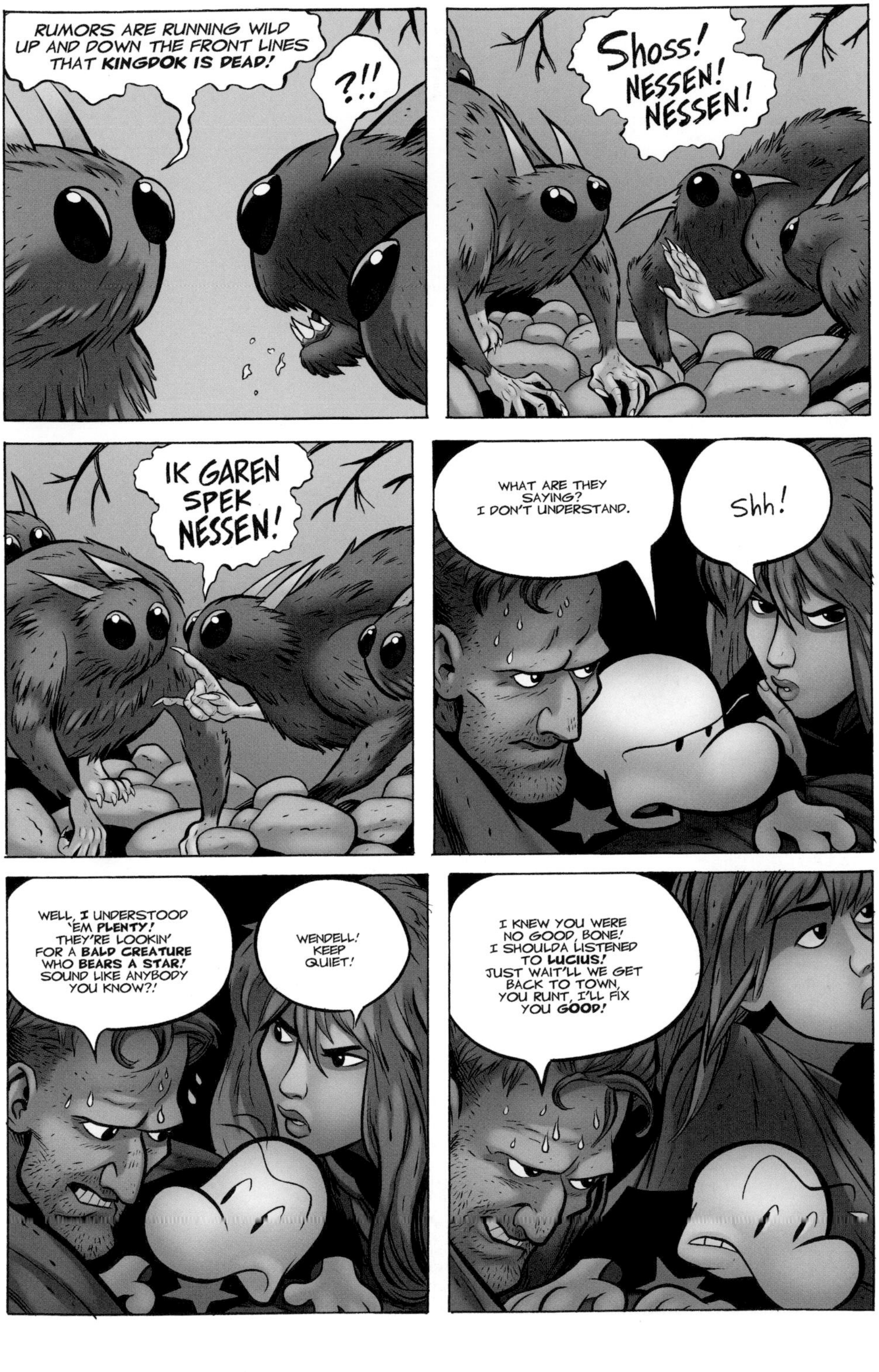
RUMORS ARE RUNNING WILD UP AND DOWN THE FRONT LINES THAT KINGDOK IS DEAD!
?!!
Shoss! NESSEN! NESSEN!
IK GAREN SPEK NESSEN!
WHAT ARE THEY SAYING? I DON'T UNDERSTAND.
Shh!
WELL, I UNDERSTOOD 'EM PLENTY! THEY'RE LOOKIN' FOR A BALD CREATURE WHO BEARS A STAR! SOUND LIKE ANYBODY YOU KNOW?!
WENDELL! KEEP QUIET!
I KNEW YOU WERE NO GOOD, BONE! I SHOULDA LISTENED TO LUCIUS! JUST WAIT'LL WE GET BACK TO TOWN, YOU RUNT, I'LL FIX YOU GOOD!

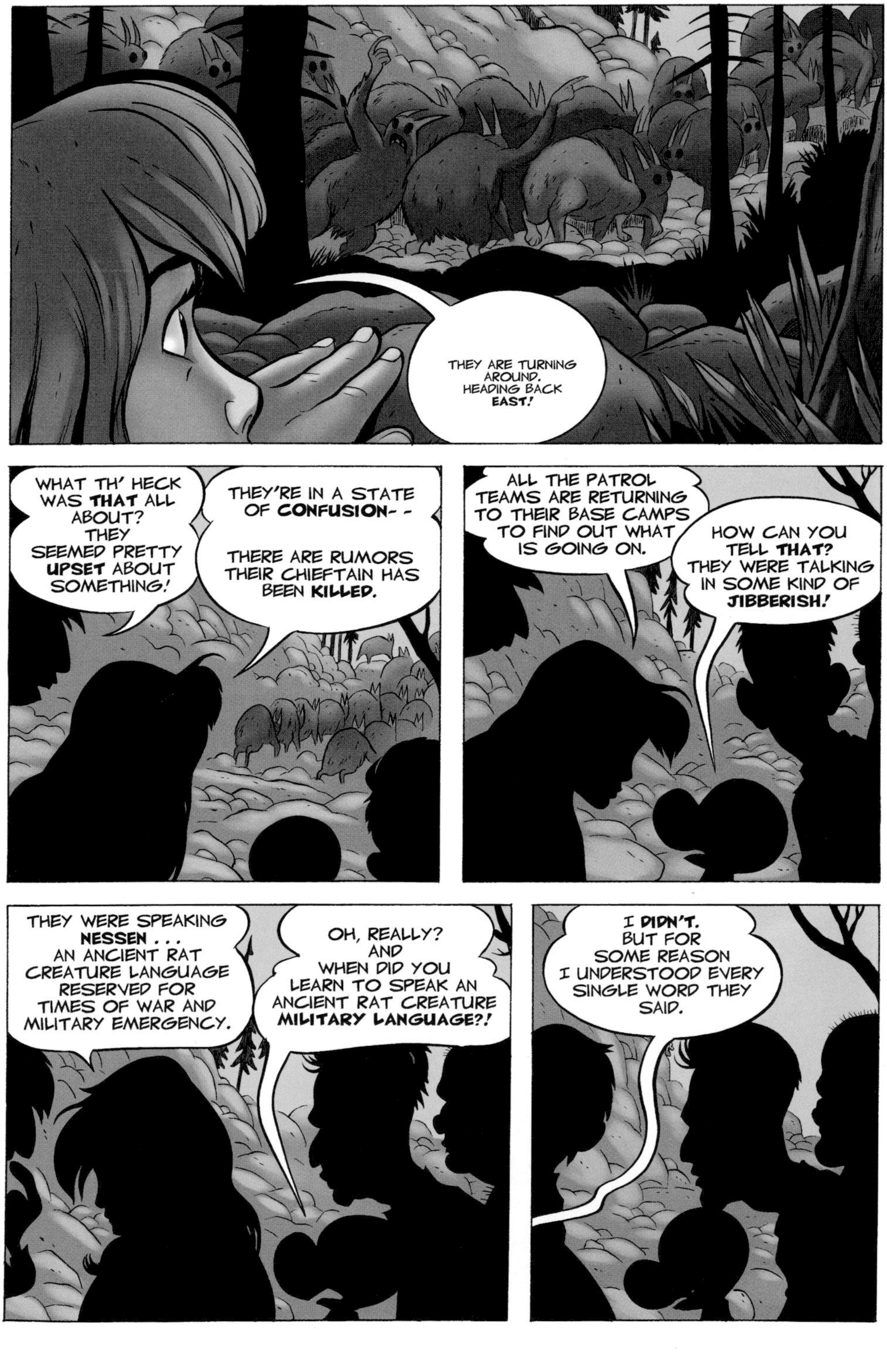
THEY ARE TURNING AROUND. HEADING BACK EAST!
WHAT TH' HECK WAS THAT ALL ABOUT? THEY SEEMED PRETTY UPSET ABOUT SOMETHING!
THEY'RE IN A STATE OF CONFUSION- -
THERE ARE RUMORS THEIR CHIEFTAIN HAS BEEN KILLED.
ALL THE PATROL TEAMS ARE RETURNING TO THEIR BASE CAMPS TO FIND OUT WHAT IS GOING ON.
HOW CAN YOU TELL THAT? THEY WERE TALKING IN SOME KIND OF JIBBERISH!
THEY WERE SPEAKING NESSEN . . . AN ANCIENT RAT CREATURE LANGUAGE RESERVED FOR TIMES OF WAR AND MILITARY EMERGENCY.
OH, REALLY? AND WHEN DID YOU LEARN TO SPEAK AN ANCIENT RAT CREATURE MILITARY LANGUAGE?!
I DIDN'T. BUT FOR SOME REASON I UNDERSTOOD EVERY SINGLE WORD THEY SAID.

OH, NO...
NO...

THIS CAN'T BE RIGHT. WE MUST'VE TAKEN A WRONG TURN.

I'M **SURE** THIS IS IT... BUT... BUT...

IT'S **GONE!** THE ENTIRE VILLAGE IS **GONE!**

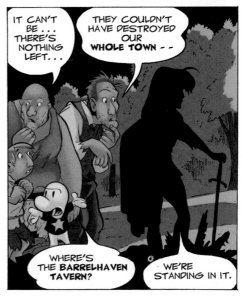

IT CAN'T BE... THERE'S NOTHING LEFT...

THEY COULDN'T HAVE DESTROYED OUR **WHOLE TOWN** --

WHERE'S THE **BARRELHAVEN** TAVERN?

WE'RE STANDING IN IT.

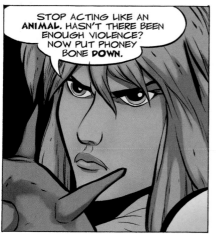

STOP ACTING LIKE AN **ANIMAL.** HASN'T THERE BEEN ENOUGH VIOLENCE? NOW PUT PHONEY BONE **DOWN.**

NO!! HE SWINDLED US AND **DESTROYED** OUR TOWN!

HE DIDN'T ATTACK THE VILLAGE! THE **RAT CREATURES** DID!

HE TRICKED US INTO CHASIN' AFTER **DRAGONS!** WE WERE AWAY FROM OUR **HOMES** WHEN WE SHOULDA BEEN **HERE** DEFENDING THE **VILLAGE!**

NOBODY **FORCED** YOU TO FOLLOW HIM! YOU WERE A **MOB** LOOKING FOR SCAPEGOATS!

BUT IF WE HAD BEEN **HERE**, THEN LUCIUS MIGHT STILL BE **ALIVE!**

WE DON'T KNOW WHAT HAPPENED TO LUCIUS... BUT WHATEVER IT WAS, IF YOU **HAD** BEEN HERE, YOU WOULD HAVE **SHARED** HIS FATE!

AND SO WOULD ALL THE OTHER VILLAGERS WHO WERE **WITH** YOU HUNTING DRAGONS! THIS BONE PROBABLY SAVED **HALF THE VILLAGE** BY TAKING YOU UP INTO THE MOUNTAINS!

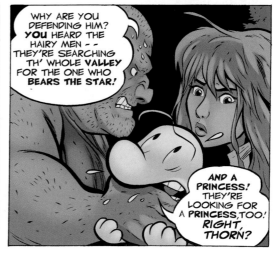

WHY ARE YOU DEFENDING HIM? **YOU** HEARD THE HAIRY MEN -- THEY'RE SEARCHING TH' WHOLE **VALLEY** FOR THE ONE WHO BEARS THE STAR!

AND A **PRINCESS!** THEY'RE LOOKING FOR A **PRINCESS,TOO!** RIGHT, **THORN?**

SHUT UP, YOU!

SCRINCH

GURK!

KEEP IT UP, EUCLID! THE MORE WE BEHAVE LIKE **BRUTES**, THE MORE POWER OUR **ENEMIES** HAVE!

WHAT DO **YOU** SAY, WENDELL? DO WE **STRING HIM UP** OR **NOT?**

I DON'T KNOW...

GIK GURK

...THIS MUCH DESTRUCTION

MAYBE THORN'S **RIGHT.** THERE'S BEEN **ENOUGH** VIOLENCE.

YOU DON'T WANNA LET HIM **OFF THE HOOK,** DO YA?

GERK!

WE'RE AS MUCH TO BLAME AS HE IS! GET **AHOLD OF** YOURSELF!

I'LL GET HOLD OF MYSELF RIGHT AFTER I **TWIST** HIS SCRAWNY NECK!

IT'S THORN!! IT'S **THORN!** SHE'S TH' **PRINCESS!!**

GO ON, YER MAJESTY, **ORDER THIS APE OFF** OF ME!

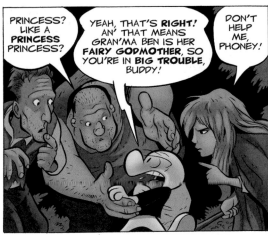

PRINCESS? LIKE A **PRINCESS** PRINCESS?

YEAH, THAT'S **RIGHT!** AN' THAT MEANS GRAN'MA BEN IS HER **FAIRY GODMOTHER,** SO YOU'RE IN **BIG TROUBLE,** BUDDY!

DON'T HELP ME, PHONEY!

THE RAT CREATURES **WERE** SEARCHING FOR A PRINCESS...

OKAY, OKAY, THE RAT CREATURES **MAY** THINK I'M A PRINCESS, **THAT** MUCH IS TRUE.

A **PRINCESS**? **HOW**? FROM **WHERE**?! THE ROYAL FAMILY WAS KILLED IN THE BIG **WAR**!

THERE HASN'T BEEN A KINGDOM FOR ALMOST **FIFTEEN YEARS**!

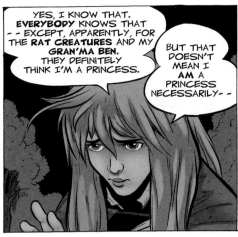

YES, I KNOW THAT. **EVERYBODY** KNOWS THAT -- EXCEPT, APPARENTLY, FOR THE **RAT CREATURES** AND MY **GRAN'MA BEN**. THEY DEFINITELY THINK I'M A PRINCESS.

BUT THAT DOESN'T MEAN I **AM** A PRINCESS NECESSARILY--

SHE DOES KINDA **LOOK** LIKE A PRINCESS.

YES, BUT WHAT DOES THAT MAKE OL' **ROSE BEN**? THE LOST QUEEN OF THE **VALLEY**? OL' **GRAN'MA BEN** RACES **COWS**, REMEMBER...

LOOK, I DON'T KNOW IF IT'S TRUE... BUT I **AM** SURE WE SHOULDN'T BE DISCUSSING IT **HERE**!

THAT MEANS **YOU** CAN JUST KEEP YOUR **TRAP SHUT** -- UNDERSTAND?

YEAH, YEAH. WE ALL GOT OUR LITTLE **DELUSIONS OF GRANDEUR**. I COULD TELL YOU WANTED TO GET IT OFF YOUR CHEST.

LISTEN UP. THIS WAR CLUB BELONGS TO MY FRIEND **FONE BONE**. I FOUND IT HERE IN THE WRECKAGE OF THE BARN, AND THERE'S A GOOD CHANCE HE AND SOME OTHERS **ESCAPED**...

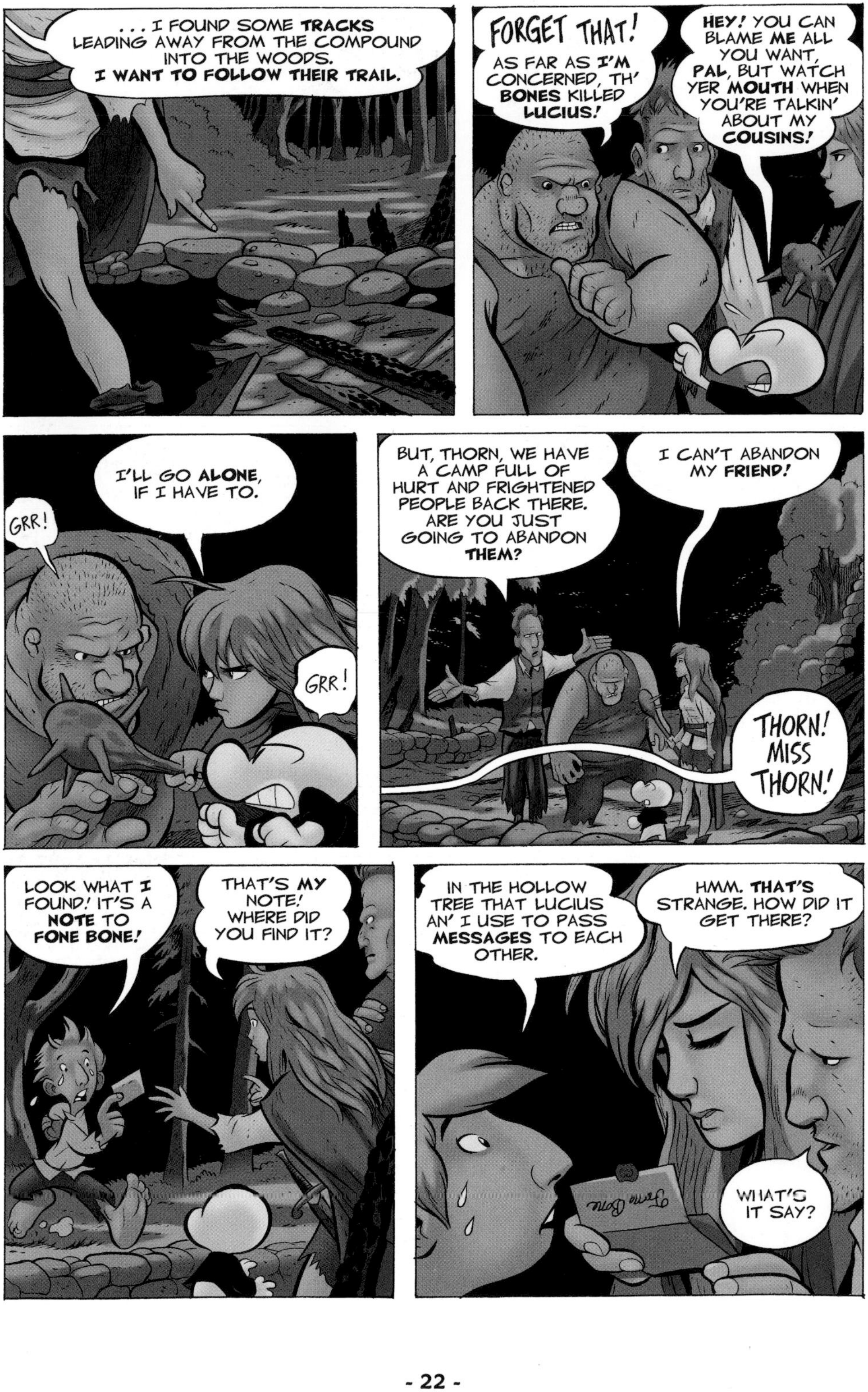
. . . I FOUND SOME TRACKS LEADING AWAY FROM THE COMPOUND INTO THE WOODS. I WANT TO FOLLOW THEIR TRAIL.
FORGET THAT!
AS FAR AS I'M CONCERNED, TH' BONES KILLED LUCIUS!
HEY! YOU CAN BLAME ME ALL YOU WANT, PAL, BUT WATCH YER MOUTH WHEN YOU'RE TALKIN' ABOUT MY COUSINS!
I'LL GO ALONE, IF I HAVE TO.
GRR!
GRR!
BUT, THORN, WE HAVE A CAMP FULL OF HURT AND FRIGHTENED PEOPLE BACK THERE. ARE YOU JUST GOING TO ABANDON THEM?
I CAN'T ABANDON MY FRIEND!
THORN! MISS THORN!
LOOK WHAT I FOUND! IT'S A NOTE TO FONE BONE!
THAT'S MY NOTE! WHERE DID YOU FIND IT?
IN THE HOLLOW TREE THAT LUCIUS AN' I USE TO PASS MESSAGES TO EACH OTHER.
HMM. THAT'S STRANGE. HOW DID IT GET THERE?
WHAT'S IT SAY?

"I HAVE GONE HOME TO GRAN'MA'S FARM."
I WROTE THIS THE NIGHT I LEFT THE COMPOUND SO FONE BONE WOULD KNOW WHERE I WENT...
Dear Fone Bone,
I have gone home to
Gran'ma's farm. Please
dont worry... just
need to sort things
out. If you leave the
valley before we see
LUCIUS MUST'VE **FOUND** THE NOTE.
AND HE PUT IT IN THE TREE FOR **YOU** TO FIND, JON.
WHY?
SNIFF.
WAIT! I KNOW!
BECAUSE **HE** WENT TO GRAN'MA BEN'S FARM TO LOOK FOR **THORN**!
BLOODY STARS!!
IF HE'S **RIGHT**, THEN LUCIUS MIGHT STILL BE **ALIVE**!
YEAH! MAYBE **ALL** OUR NEIGHBORS ARE STILL ALIVE!
FIRST THING IN THE MORNING, WE HEAD NORTH TO GRAN'MA BEN'S PLACE.
RIGHT!
YOU GO.
I HAVE TO LOOK FOR FONE BONE. WILL YOU BE COMING WITH ME, PHONCIBLE?
WHO **ME**? YOU MEAN OUT **THERE?!**
GULP.
EEh.
YEAH... I'LL GO...
WELL, AT LEAST YOU'RE NOT A **COWARD!**
OR ARE YOU **MORE** AFRAID TO BE LEFT WITH **THEM**?

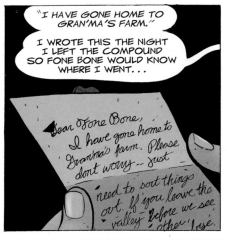

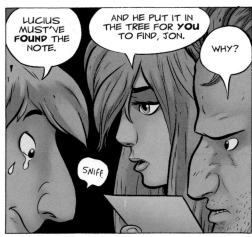

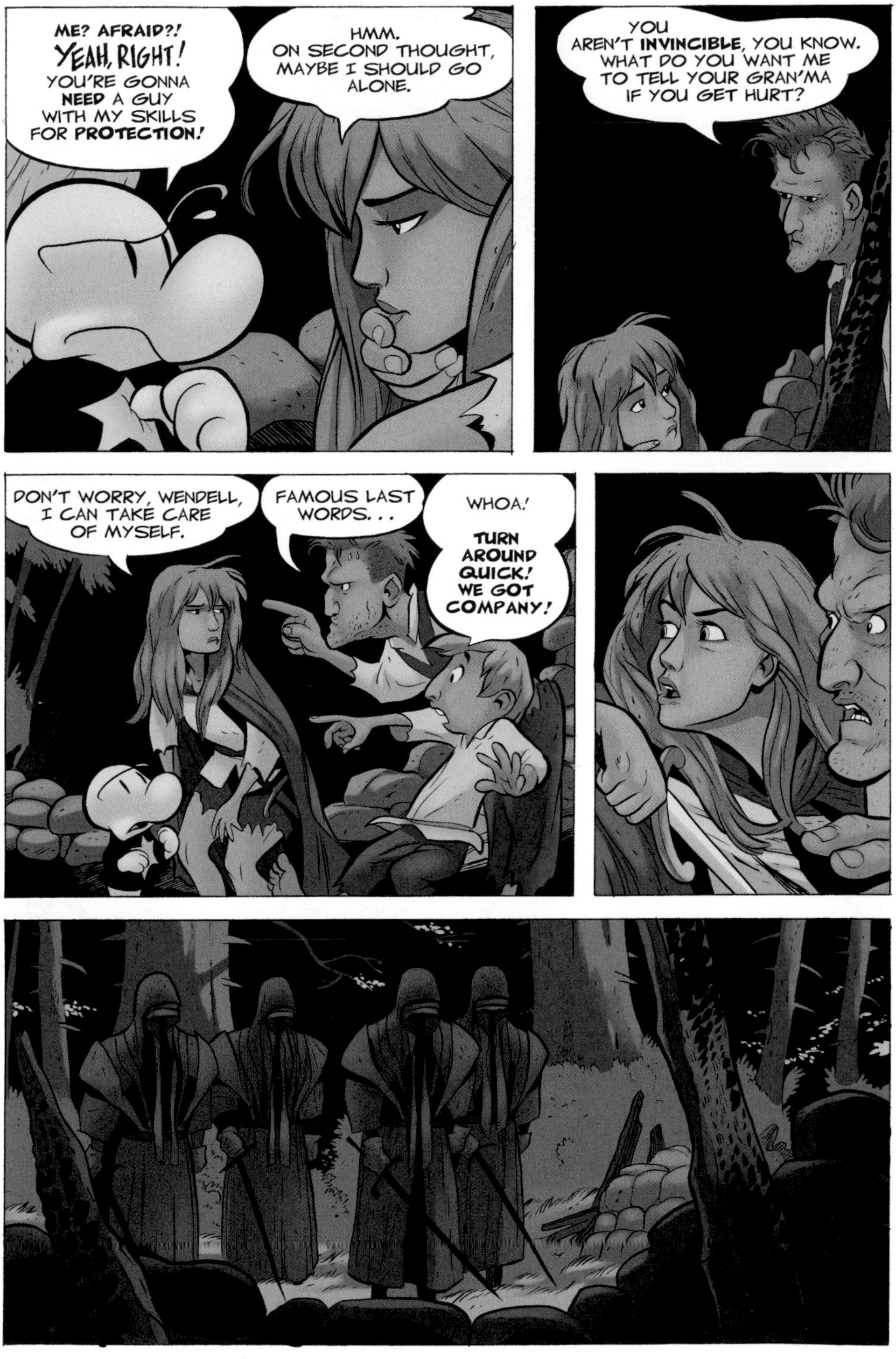
ME? AFRAID?! YEAH, RIGHT! YOU'RE GONNA NEED A GUY WITH MY SKILLS FOR PROTECTION!
HMM. ON SECOND THOUGHT, MAYBE I SHOULD GO ALONE.
YOU AREN'T INVINCIBLE, YOU KNOW. WHAT DO YOU WANT ME TO TELL YOUR GRAN'MA IF YOU GET HURT?
DON'T WORRY, WENDELL, I CAN TAKE CARE OF MYSELF.
FAMOUS LAST WORDS. . .
WHOA!
TURN AROUND QUICK! WE GOT COMPANY!

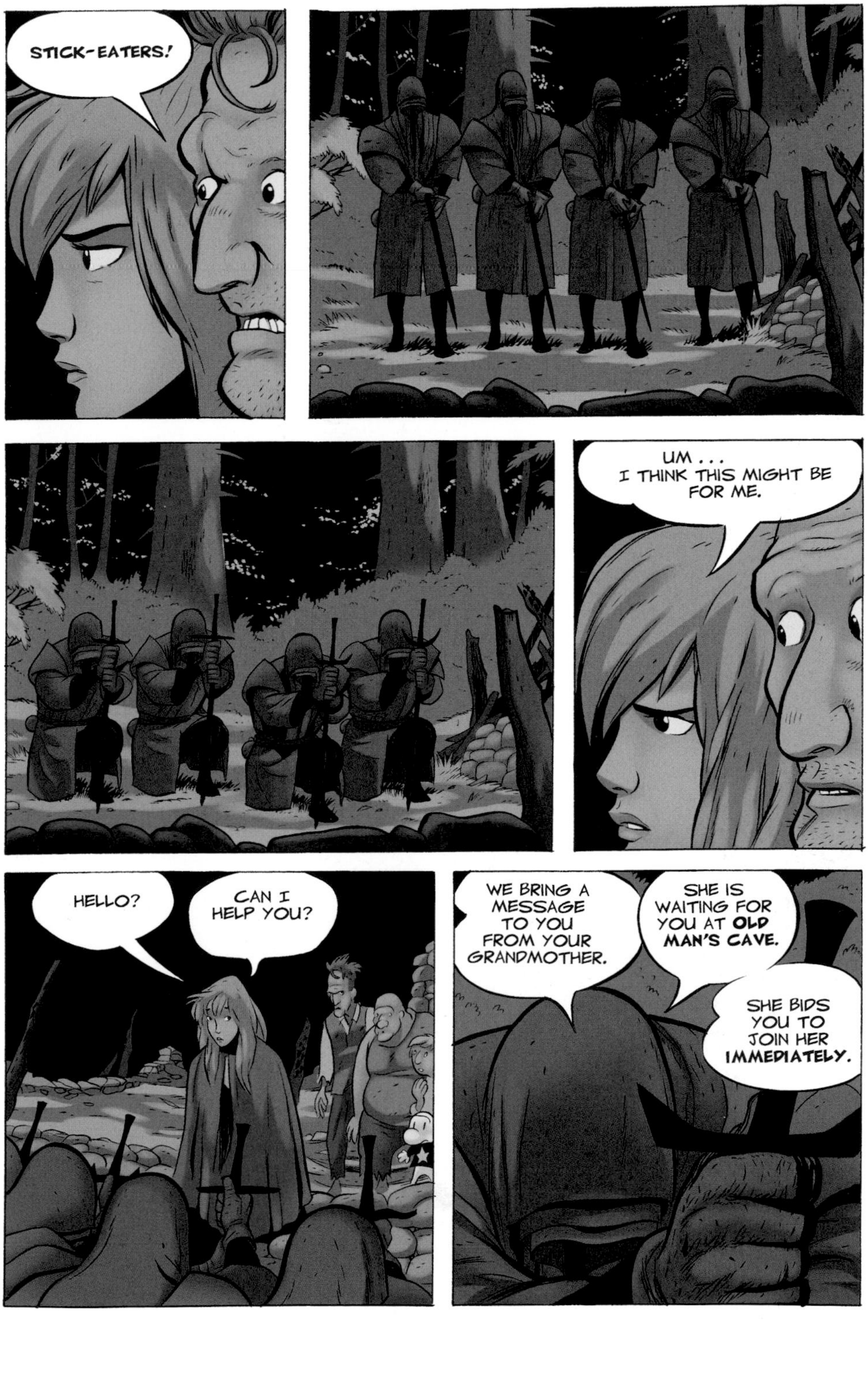
STICK-EATERS!
UM . . . I THINK THIS MIGHT BE FOR ME.
HELLO?
CAN I HELP YOU?
WE BRING A MESSAGE TO YOU FROM YOUR GRANDMOTHER.
SHE IS WAITING FOR YOU AT OLD MAN'S CAVE.
SHE BIDS YOU TO JOIN HER IMMEDIATELY.

OLD MAN'S CAVE...

HOW DO I KNOW I CAN TRUST YOU?

BEFORE I CAN GO TO OLD MAN'S CAVE, I MUST FIND MY FRIEND **FONE BONE**.

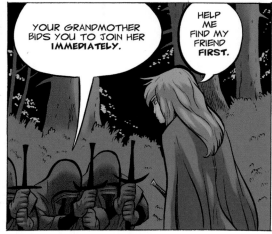

YOUR GRANDMOTHER BIDS YOU TO JOIN HER **IMMEDIATELY**.

HELP ME FIND MY FRIEND **FIRST**.

YOU **HAVE** TO HELP ME, DON'T YOU? IT IS YOUR **DUTY**.

WE ARE BUT GUIDES.

YOU ALONE MAY WALK YOUR PATH.

THEN GUIDE ME. SHOULD I SEARCH FOR MY **FRIEND**? OR SHOULD I GO TO **OLD MAN'S CAVE**?

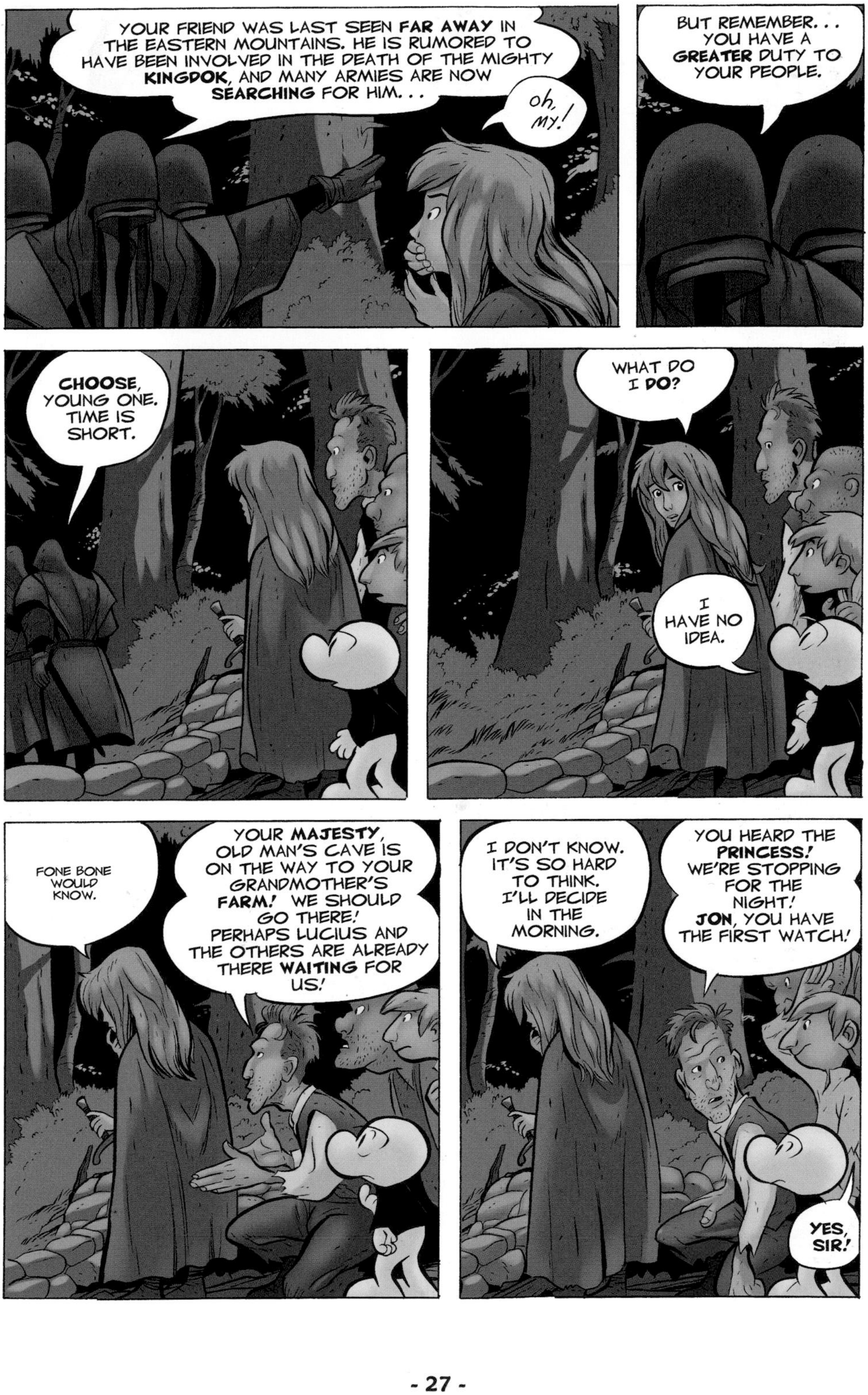
YOUR FRIEND WAS LAST SEEN FAR AWAY IN THE EASTERN MOUNTAINS. HE IS RUMORED TO HAVE BEEN INVOLVED IN THE DEATH OF THE MIGHTY KINGDOK, AND MANY ARMIES ARE NOW SEARCHING FOR HIM. . .
oh, my!
BUT REMEMBER. . . YOU HAVE A GREATER DUTY TO YOUR PEOPLE.
CHOOSE, YOUNG ONE. TIME IS SHORT.
WHAT DO I DO?
I HAVE NO IDEA.
FONE BONE WOULD KNOW.
YOUR MAJESTY, OLD MAN'S CAVE IS ON THE WAY TO YOUR GRANDMOTHER'S FARM! WE SHOULD GO THERE! PERHAPS LUCIUS AND THE OTHERS ARE ALREADY THERE WAITING FOR US!
I DON'T KNOW. IT'S SO HARD TO THINK. I'LL DECIDE IN THE MORNING.
YOU HEARD THE PRINCESS! WE'RE STOPPING FOR THE NIGHT! JON, YOU HAVE THE FIRST WATCH!
YES, SIR!

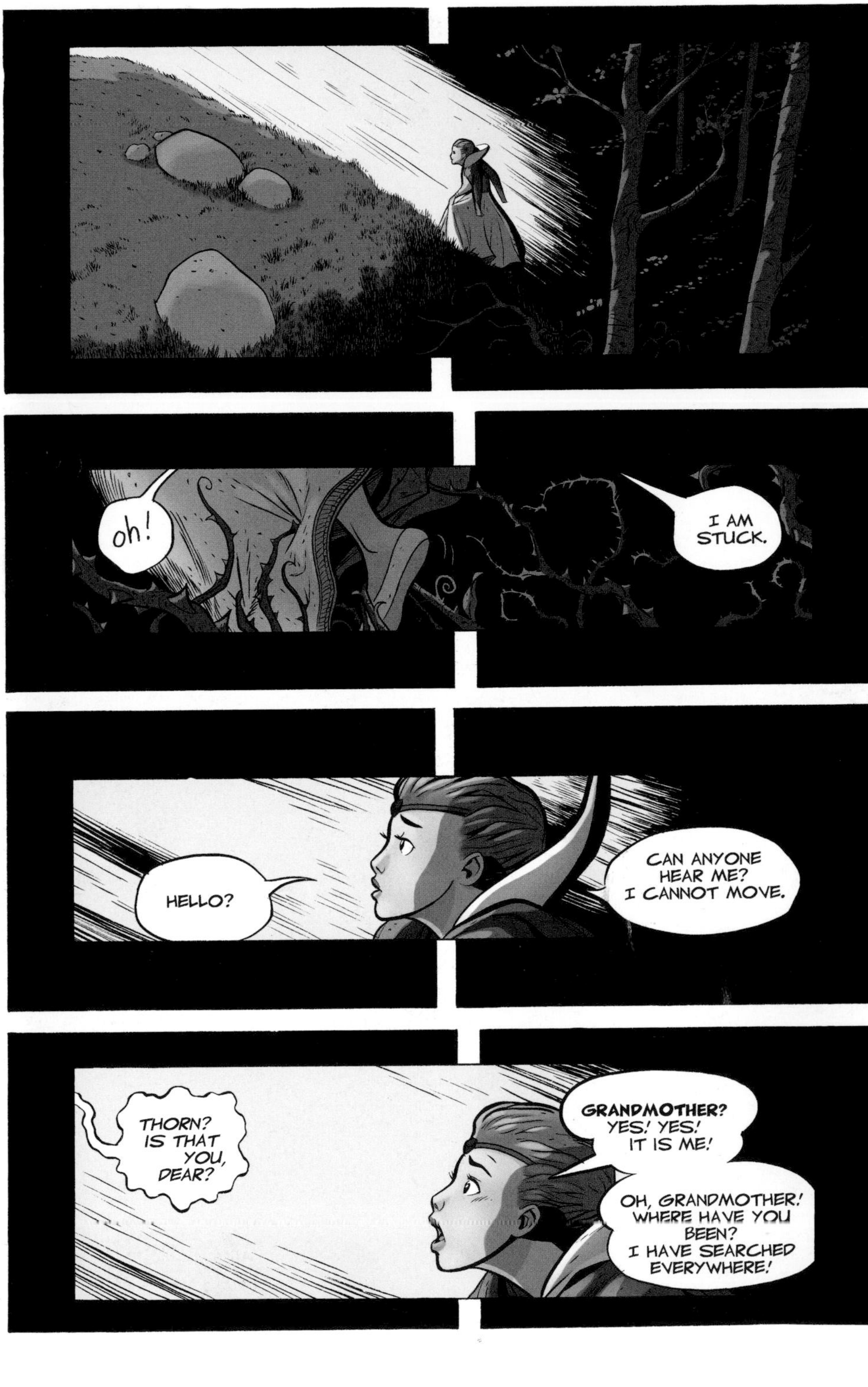
oh!
I AM STUCK.
HELLO?
CAN ANYONE HEAR ME? I CANNOT MOVE.
THORN? IS THAT YOU, DEAR?
GRANDMOTHER? YES! YES! IT IS ME!
OH, GRANDMOTHER! WHERE HAVE YOU BEEN? I HAVE SEARCHED EVERYWHERE!

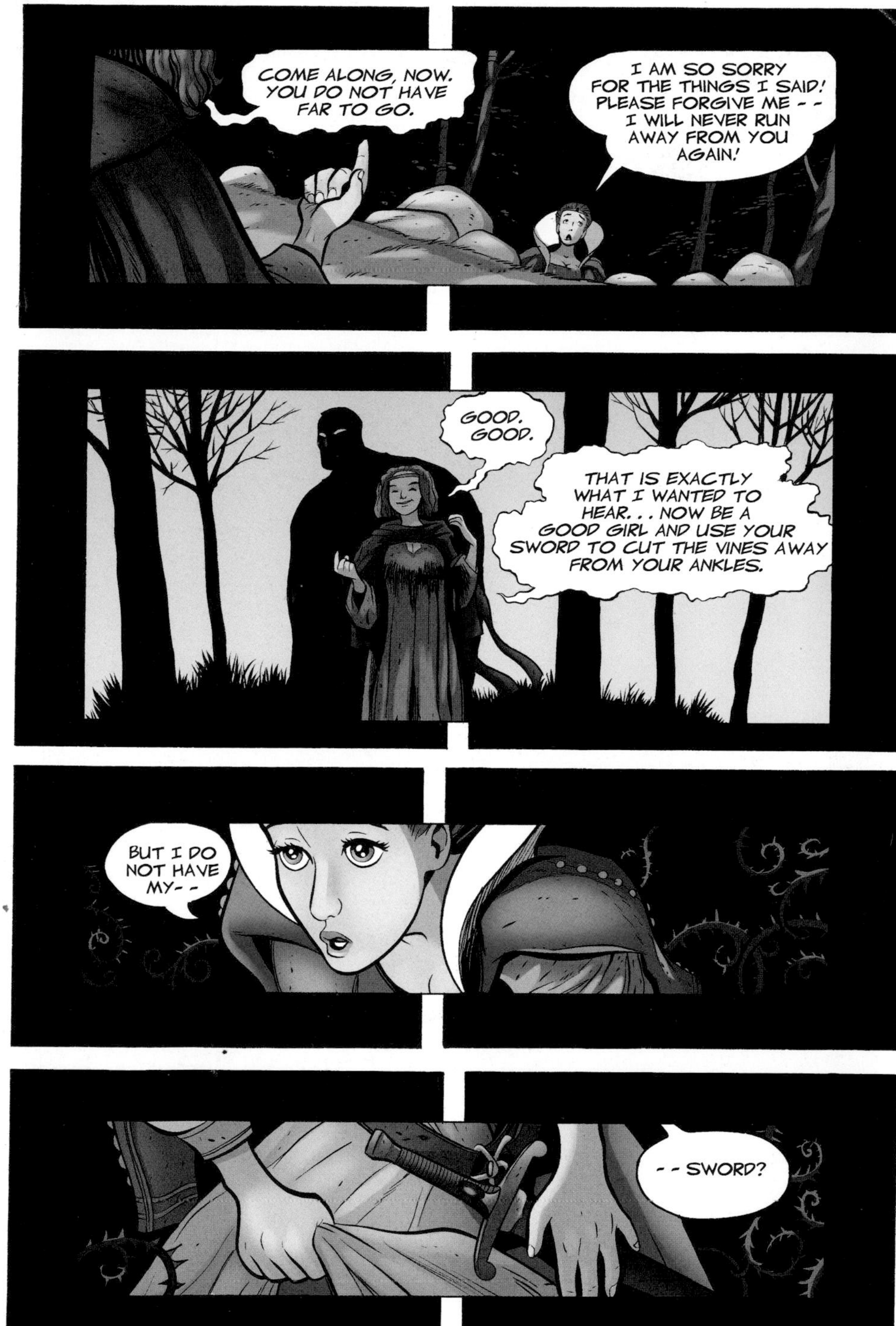
COME ALONG, NOW. YOU DO NOT HAVE FAR TO GO.
I AM SO SORRY FOR THE THINGS I SAID! PLEASE FORGIVE ME - - I WILL NEVER RUN AWAY FROM YOU AGAIN!
GOOD. GOOD.
THAT IS EXACTLY WHAT I WANTED TO HEAR. . . NOW BE A GOOD GIRL AND USE YOUR SWORD TO CUT THE VINES AWAY FROM YOUR ANKLES.
BUT I DO NOT HAVE MY- -
- - SWORD?

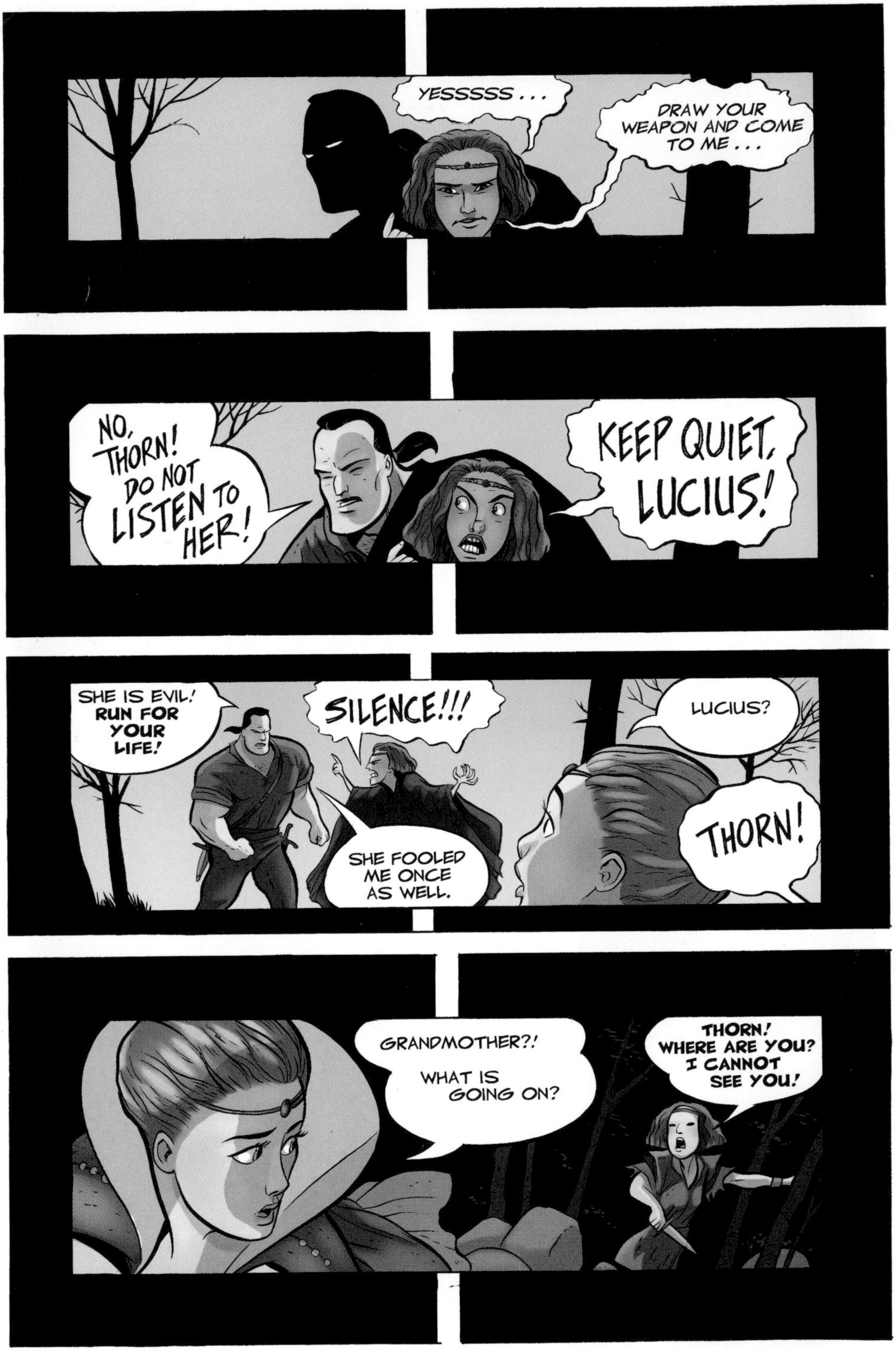
YESSSSS . . .
DRAW YOUR WEAPON AND COME TO ME . . .
NO, THORN! DO NOT LISTEN TO HER!
KEEP QUIET, LUCIUS!
SHE IS EVIL! RUN FOR YOUR LIFE!
SILENCE!!!
SHE FOOLED ME ONCE AS WELL.
LUCIUS?
THORN!
GRANDMOTHER?!
WHAT IS GOING ON?
THORN! WHERE ARE YOU? I CANNOT SEE YOU!

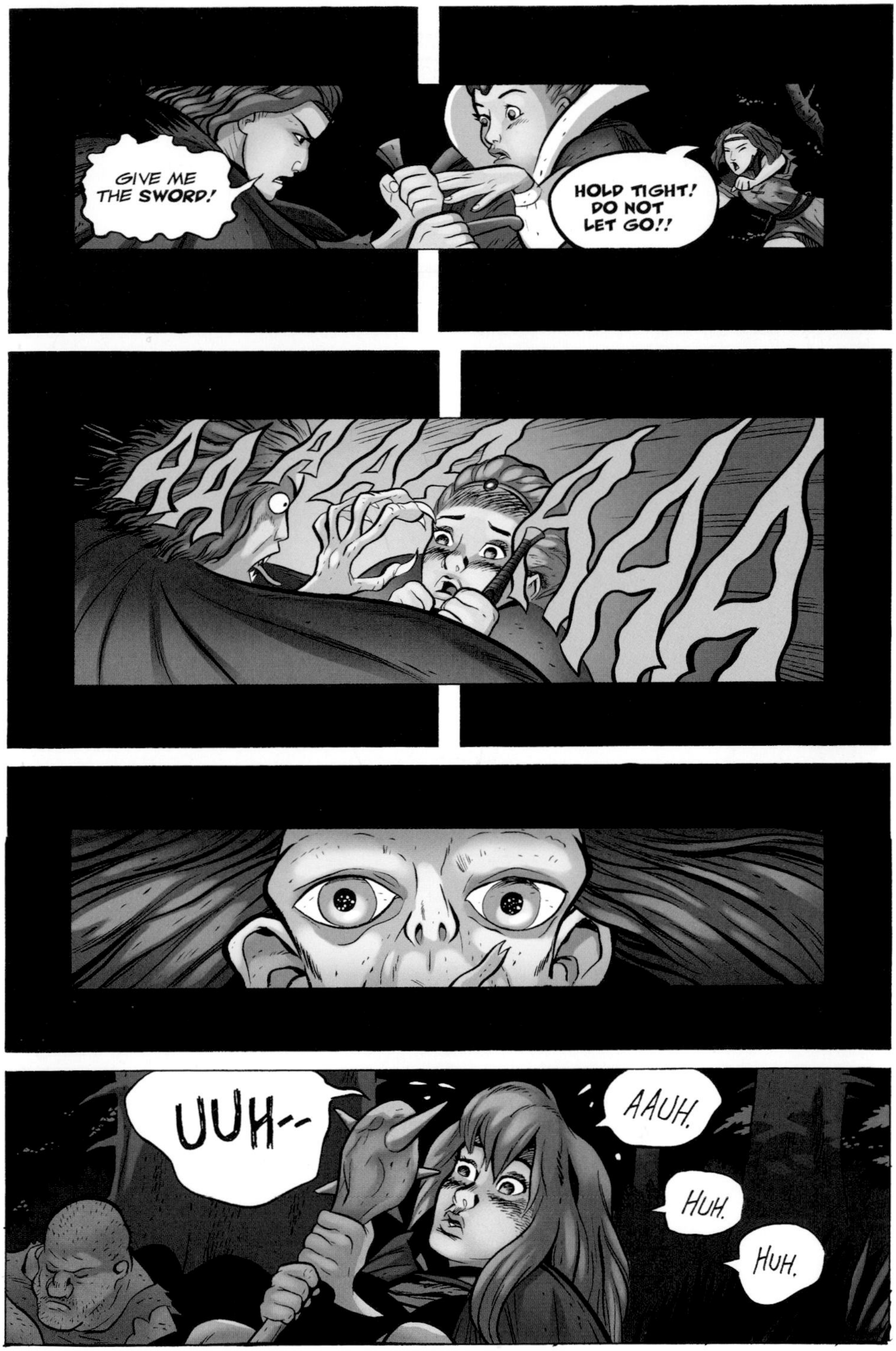
GIVE ME THE **SWORD!**
HOLD TIGHT! DO NOT LET GO!!
AAAAAAAAAAAA
UUH--
AAUH.
HUH.
HUH.

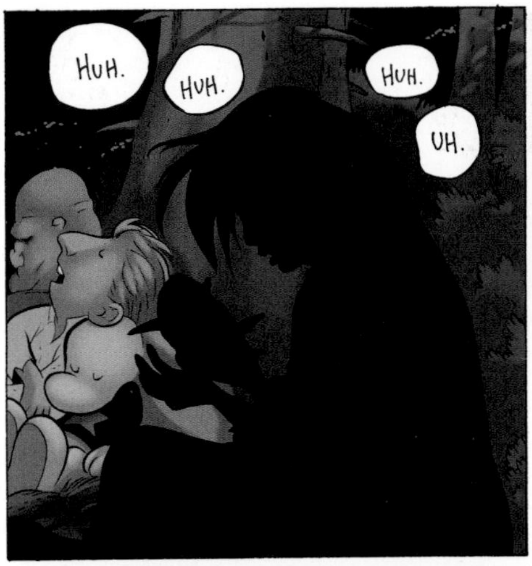
HUH.
HUH.
HUH.
UH.

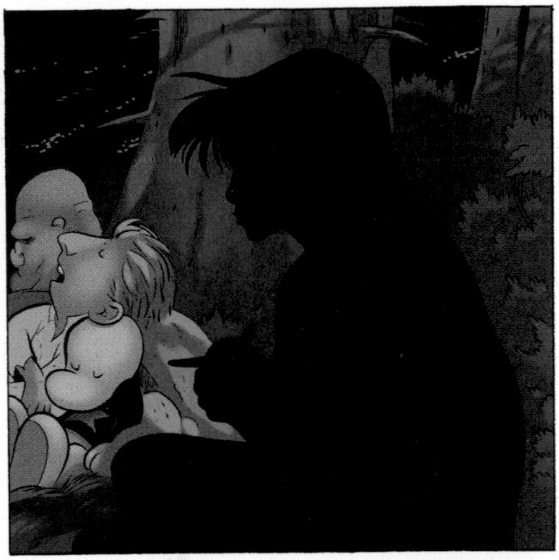

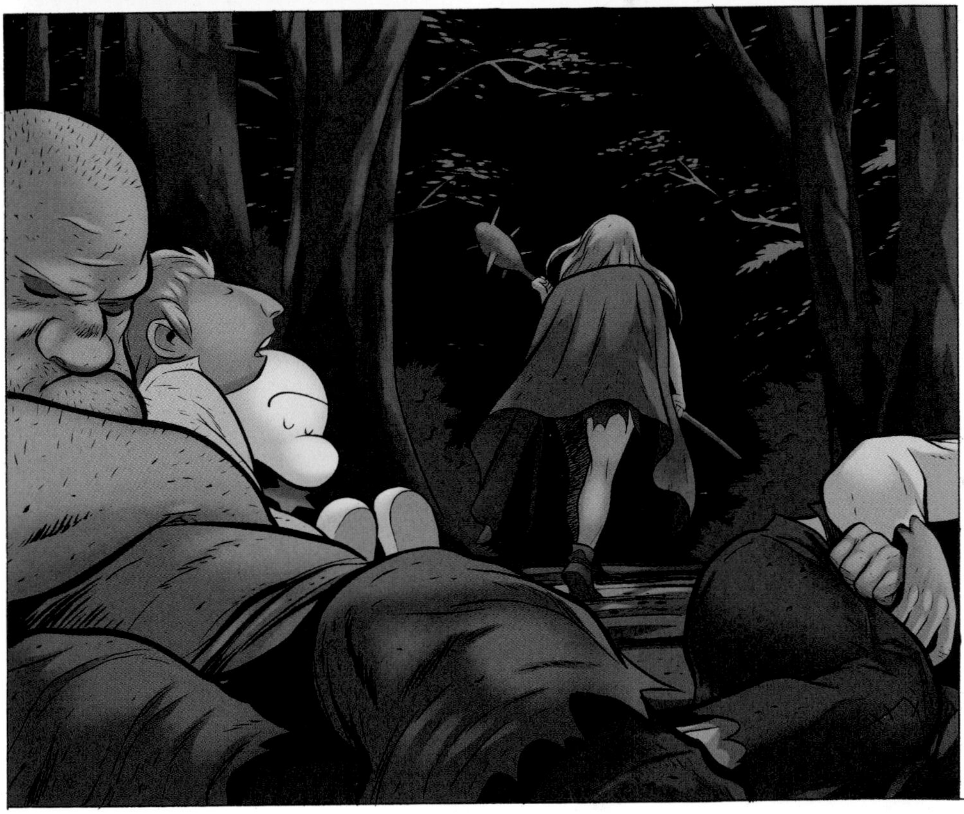

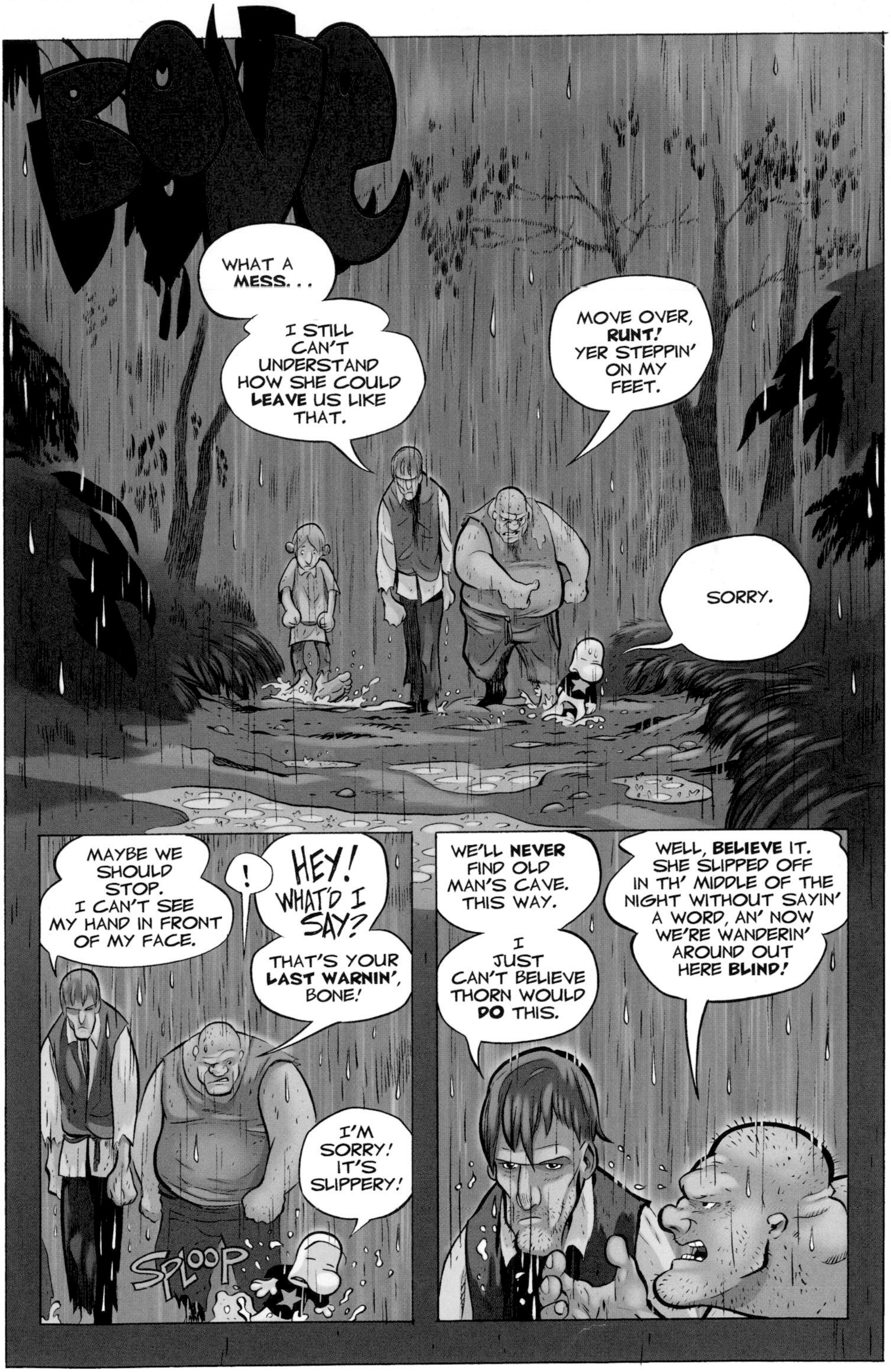
BONE
WHAT A MESS. . .
I STILL CAN'T UNDERSTAND HOW SHE COULD LEAVE US LIKE THAT.
MOVE OVER, RUNT! YER STEPPIN' ON MY FEET.
SORRY.
MAYBE WE SHOULD STOP. I CAN'T SEE MY HAND IN FRONT OF MY FACE.
!
HEY! WHAT'D I SAY?
THAT'S YOUR LAST WARNIN', BONE!
I'M SORRY! IT'S SLIPPERY!
SPLOOP
WE'LL NEVER FIND OLD MAN'S CAVE. THIS WAY.
I JUST CAN'T BELIEVE THORN WOULD DO THIS.
WELL, BELIEVE IT. SHE SLIPPED OFF IN TH' MIDDLE OF THE NIGHT WITHOUT SAYIN' A WORD, AN' NOW WE'RE WANDERIN' AROUND OUT HERE BLIND!

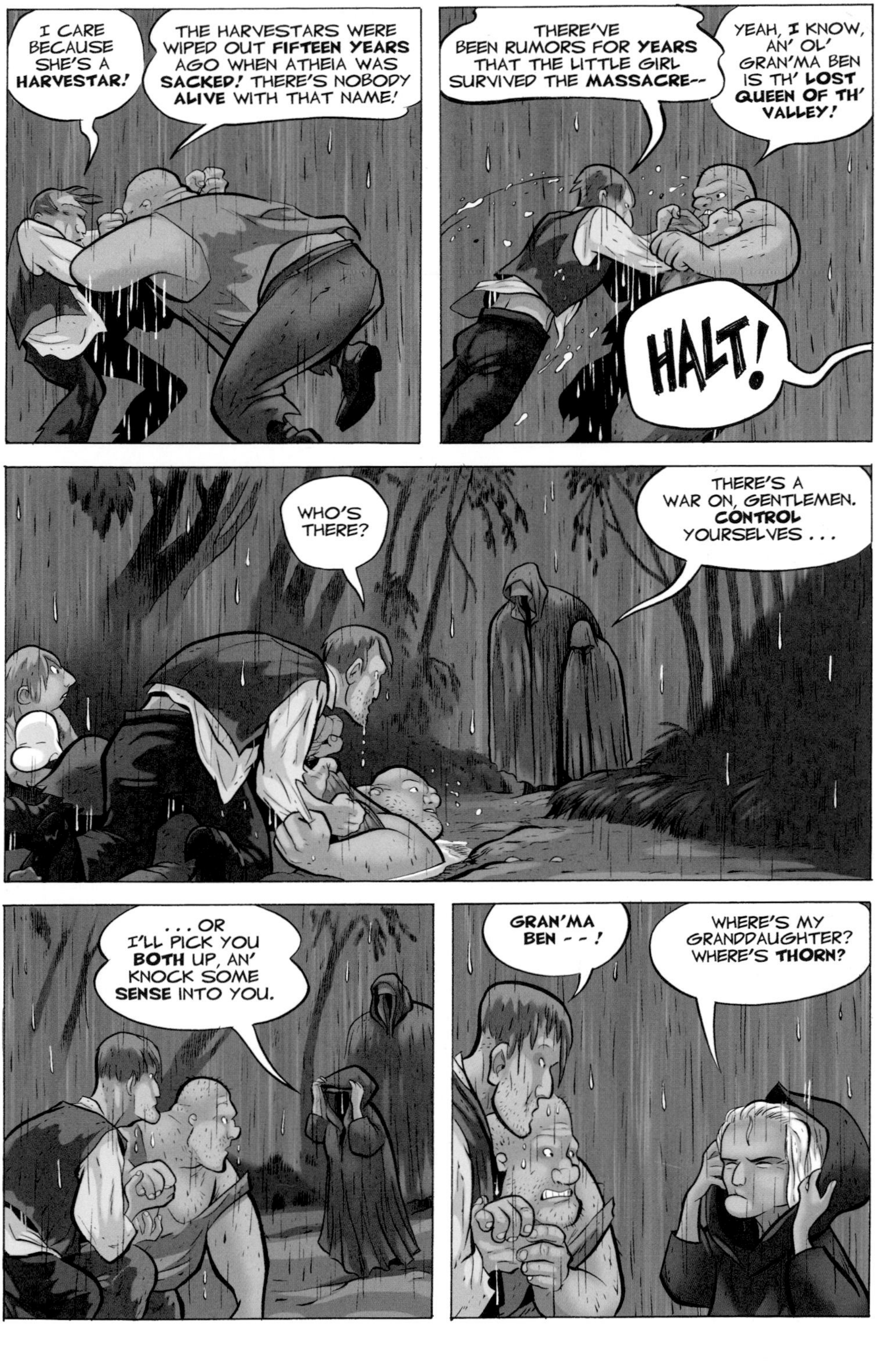
I CARE BECAUSE SHE'S A **HARVESTAR!**
THE HARVESTARS WERE WIPED OUT **FIFTEEN YEARS** AGO WHEN ATHEIA WAS **SACKED!** THERE'S NOBODY **ALIVE** WITH THAT NAME!
THERE'VE BEEN RUMORS FOR **YEARS** THAT THE LITTLE GIRL SURVIVED THE **MASSACRE--**
YEAH, **I KNOW,** AN' OL' GRAN'MA BEN IS TH' **LOST QUEEN OF TH' VALLEY!**
HALT!
WHO'S THERE?
THERE'S A WAR ON, GENTLEMEN. **CONTROL** YOURSELVES . . .
. . . OR I'LL PICK YOU **BOTH** UP, AN' KNOCK SOME **SENSE** INTO YOU.
GRAN'MA BEN - - !
WHERE'S MY GRANDDAUGHTER? WHERE'S **THORN?**

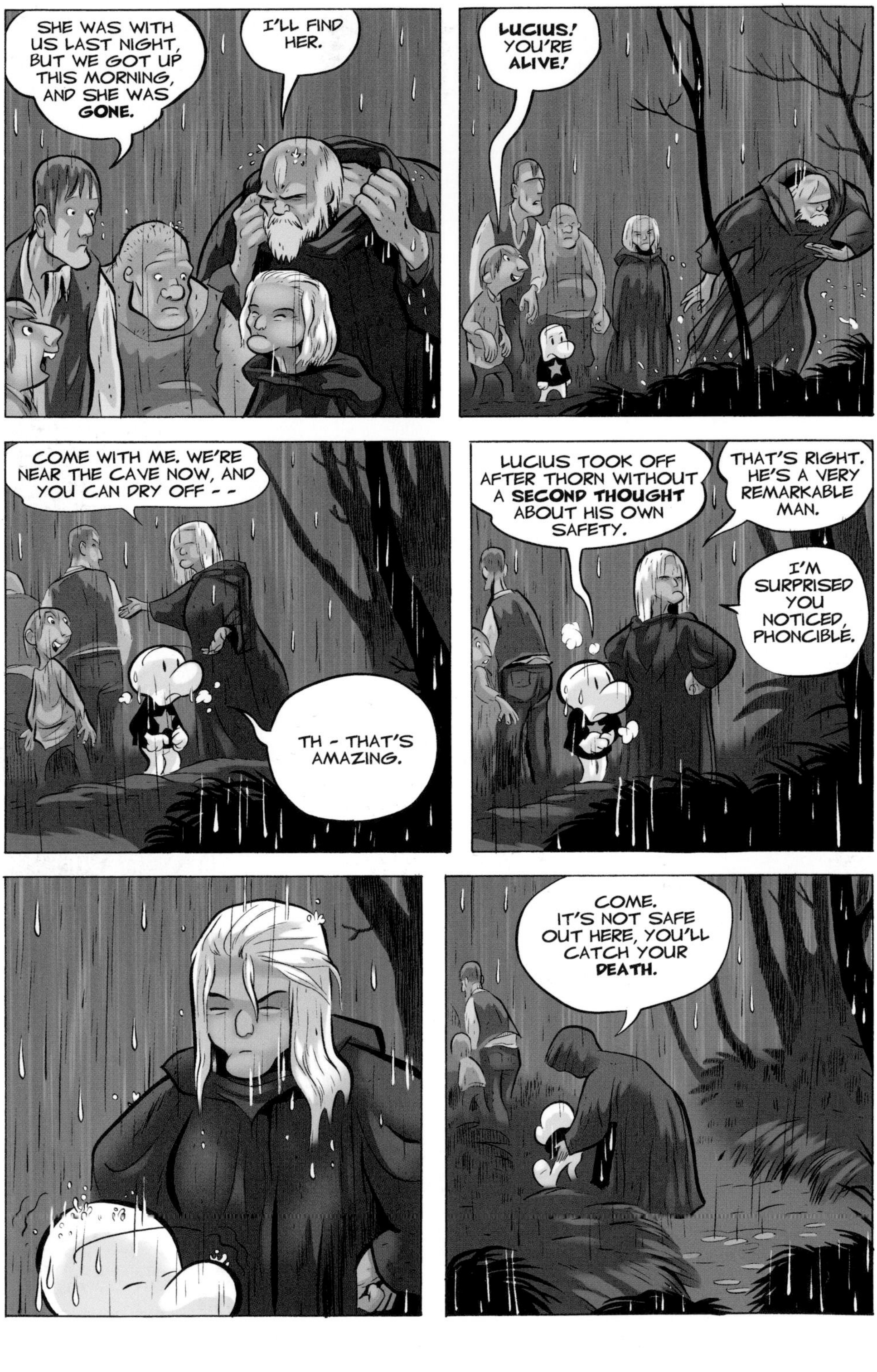
SHE WAS WITH US LAST NIGHT, BUT WE GOT UP THIS MORNING, AND SHE WAS **GONE.**
I'LL FIND HER.
LUCIUS! YOU'RE **ALIVE!**
COME WITH ME. WE'RE NEAR THE CAVE NOW, AND YOU CAN DRY OFF - -
TH - THAT'S AMAZING.
LUCIUS TOOK OFF AFTER THORN WITHOUT A **SECOND THOUGHT** ABOUT HIS OWN SAFETY.
THAT'S RIGHT. HE'S A VERY REMARKABLE MAN.
I'M SURPRISED YOU NOTICED, PHONCIBLE.
COME. IT'S NOT SAFE OUT HERE, YOU'LL CATCH YOUR **DEATH.**

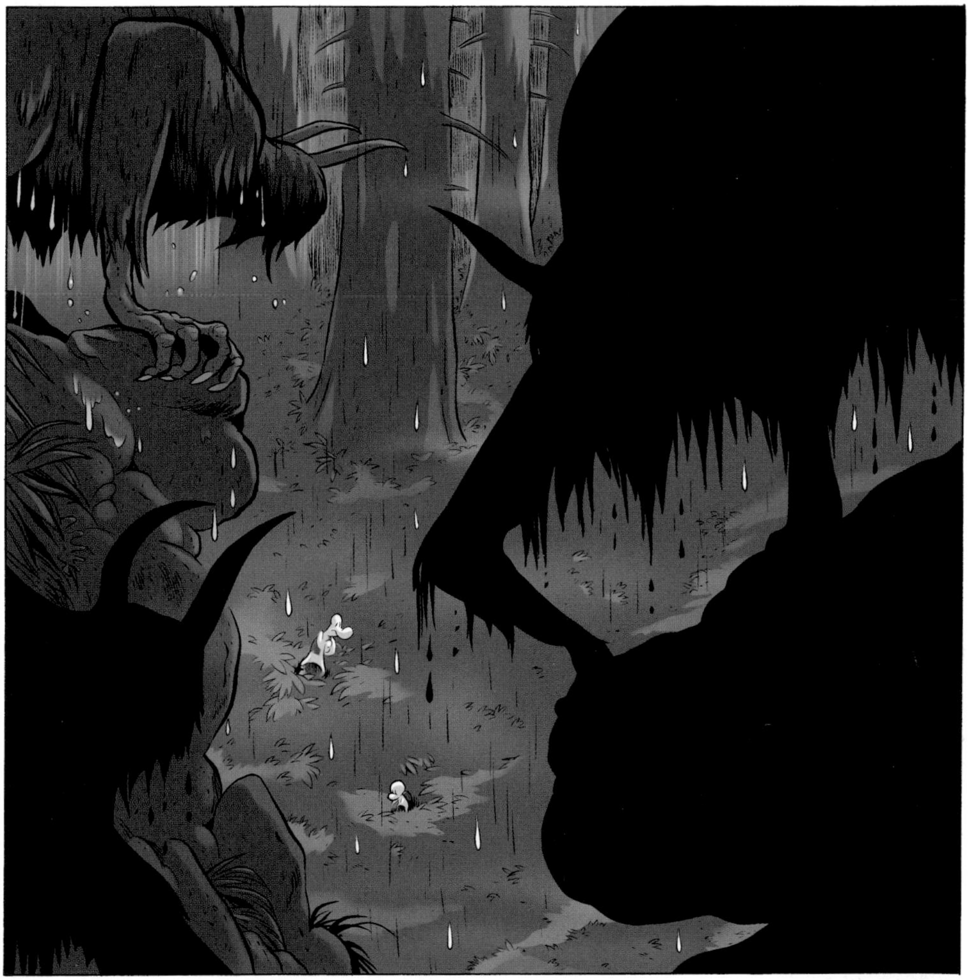

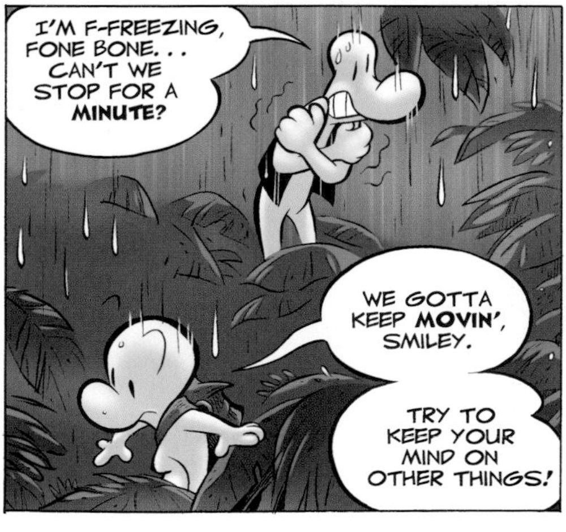
I'M F-FREEZING, FONE BONE. . . CAN'T WE STOP FOR A **MINUTE?**
WE GOTTA KEEP **MOVIN'**, SMILEY.
TRY TO KEEP YOUR MIND ON OTHER THINGS!

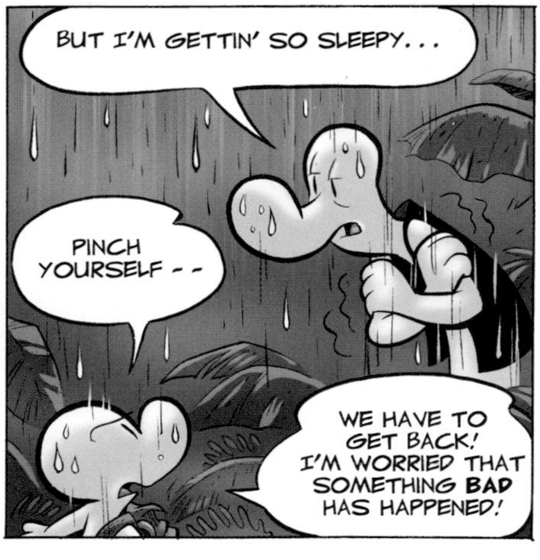
BUT I'M GETTIN' SO SLEEPY. . .
PINCH YOURSELF - -
WE HAVE TO GET BACK! I'M WORRIED THAT SOMETHING **BAD** HAS HAPPENED!

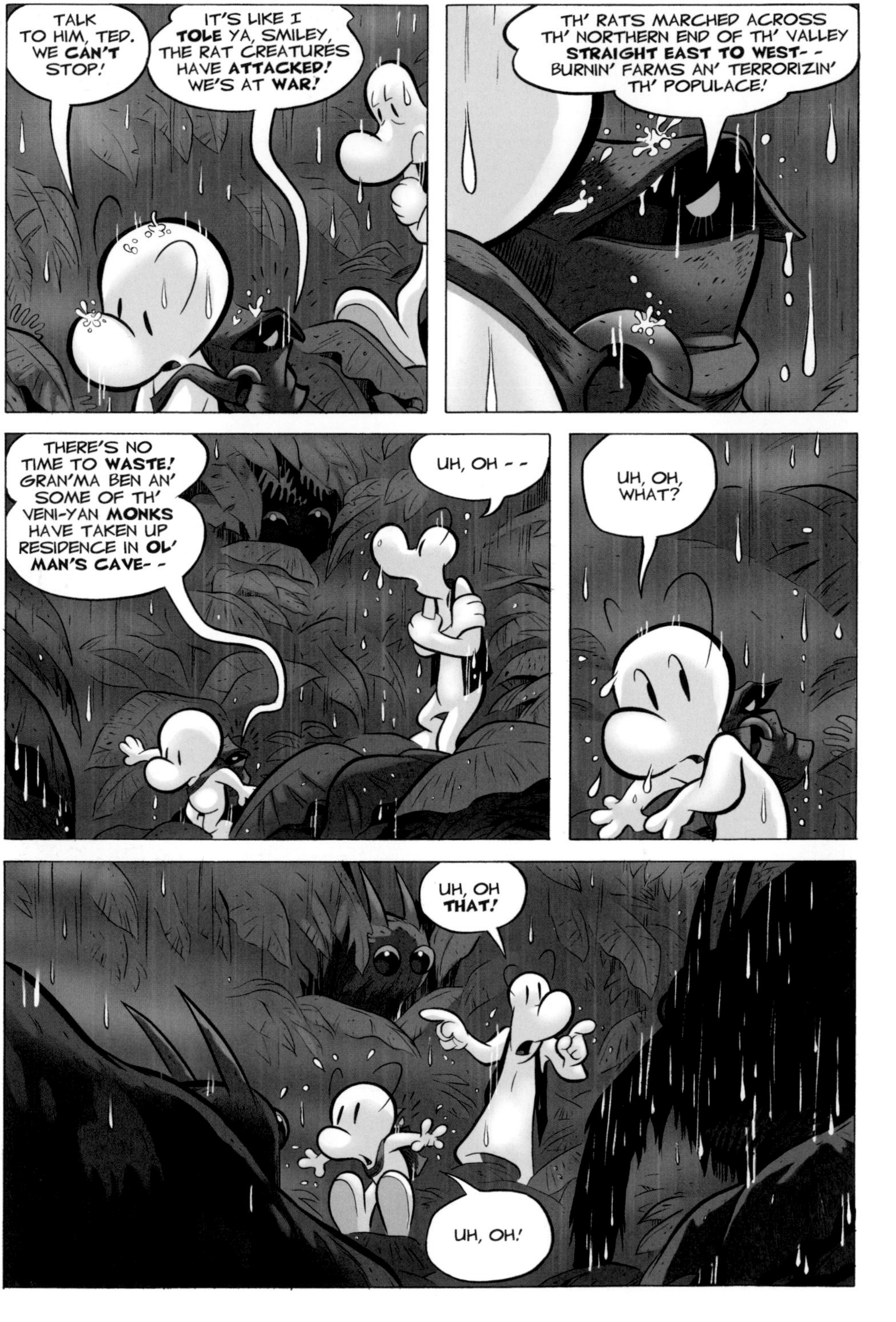
TALK TO HIM, TED. WE CAN'T STOP!
IT'S LIKE I TOLE YA, SMILEY, THE RAT CREATURES HAVE ATTACKED! WE'S AT WAR!
TH' RATS MARCHED ACROSS TH' NORTHERN END OF TH' VALLEY STRAIGHT EAST TO WEST- - BURNIN' FARMS AN' TERRORIZIN' TH' POPULACE!
THERE'S NO TIME TO WASTE! GRAN'MA BEN AN' SOME OF TH' VENI-YAN MONKS HAVE TAKEN UP RESIDENCE IN OL' MAN'S CAVE- -
UH, OH - -
UH, OH, WHAT?
UH, OH THAT!
UH, OH!

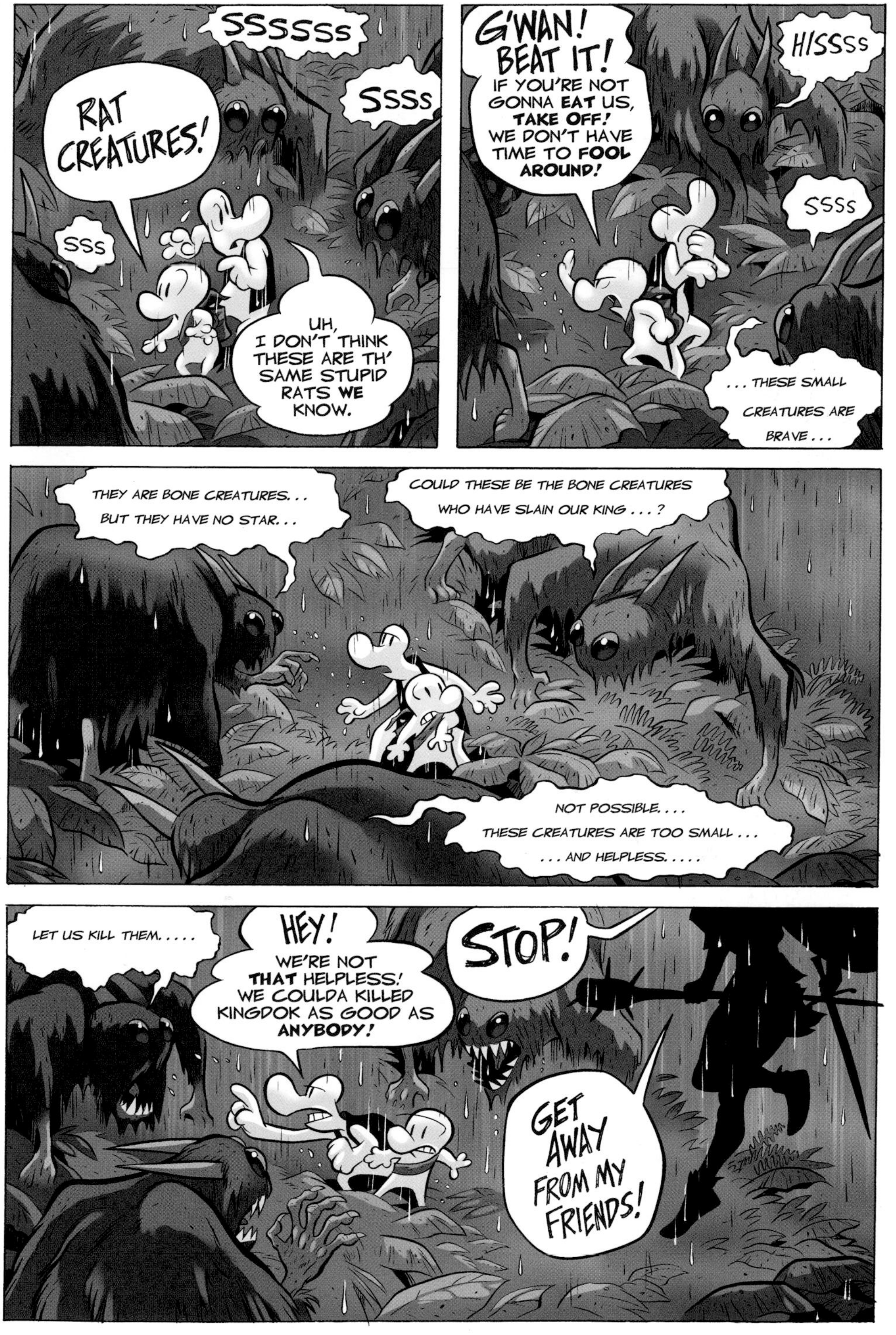
SSSSSS
RAT CREATURES!
SSSS
SSS
UH, I DON'T THINK THESE ARE TH' SAME STUPID RATS WE KNOW.
G'WAN! BEAT IT! IF YOU'RE NOT GONNA EAT US, TAKE OFF! WE DON'T HAVE TIME TO FOOL AROUND!
HISSSS
SSSS
. . . THESE SMALL CREATURES ARE BRAVE . . .
THEY ARE BONE CREATURES. . . BUT THEY HAVE NO STAR. . .
COULD THESE BE THE BONE CREATURES WHO HAVE SLAIN OUR KING . . . ?
NOT POSSIBLE. . . . THESE CREATURES ARE TOO SMALL . . . . . . AND HELPLESS. . . . .
LET US KILL THEM. . . . .
HEY! WE'RE NOT THAT HELPLESS! WE COULDA KILLED KINGDOK AS GOOD AS ANYBODY!
STOP!
GET AWAY FROM MY FRIENDS!

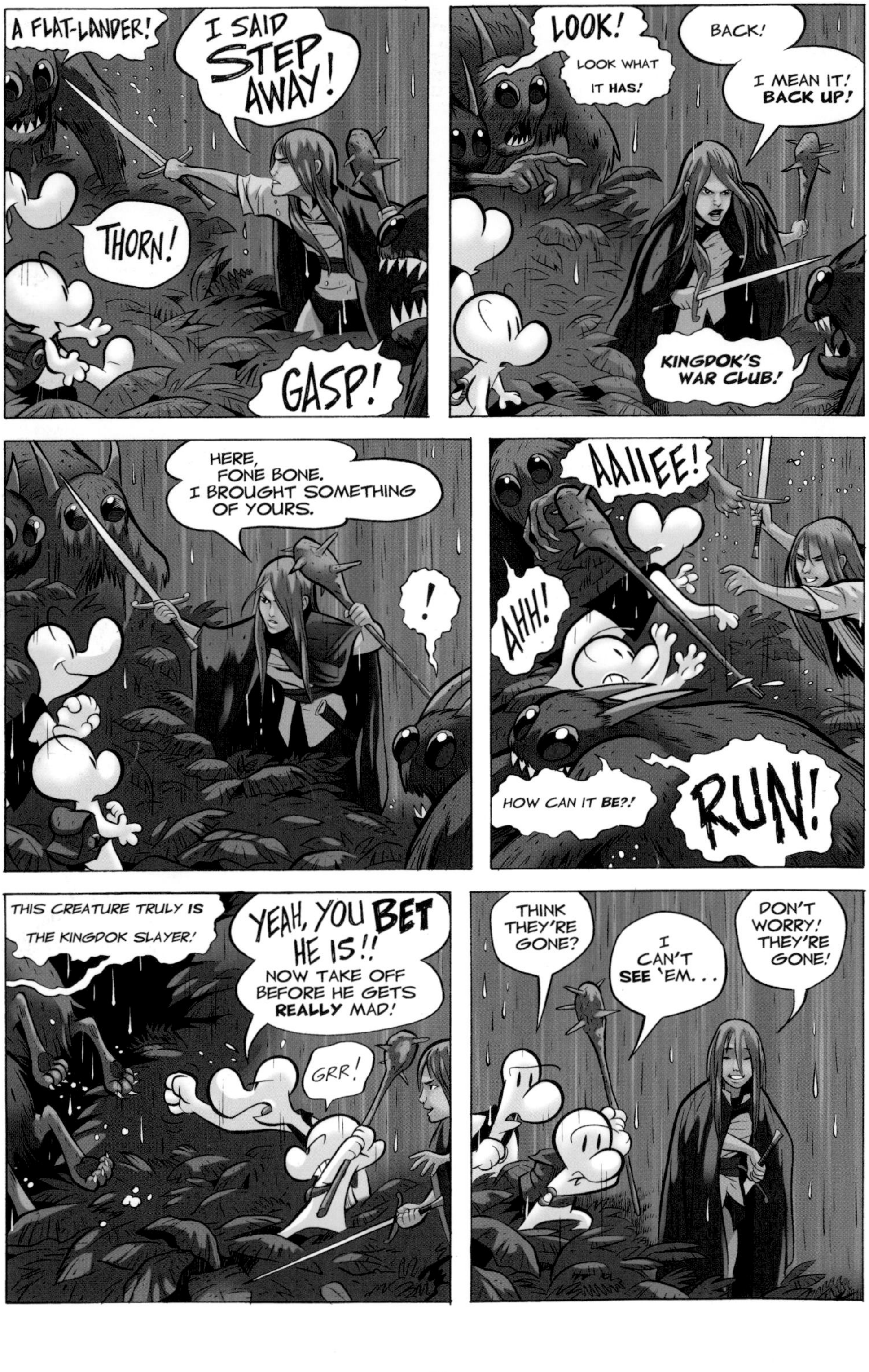
A FLAT-LANDER!
I SAID STEP AWAY!
THORN!
GASP!
LOOK!
LOOK WHAT IT HAS!
BACK!
I MEAN IT! BACK UP!
KINGDOK'S WAR CLUB!
HERE, FONE BONE. I BROUGHT SOMETHING OF YOURS.
!
AAIIEE!
AHH!
HOW CAN IT BE?!
RUN!
THIS CREATURE TRULY IS THE KINGDOK SLAYER!
YEAH, YOU BET HE IS!! NOW TAKE OFF BEFORE HE GETS REALLY MAD!
GRR!
THINK THEY'RE GONE?
I CAN'T SEE 'EM. . .
DON'T WORRY! THEY'RE GONE!

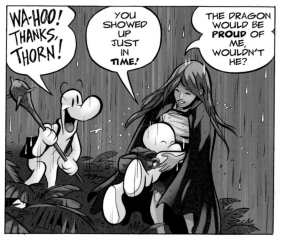

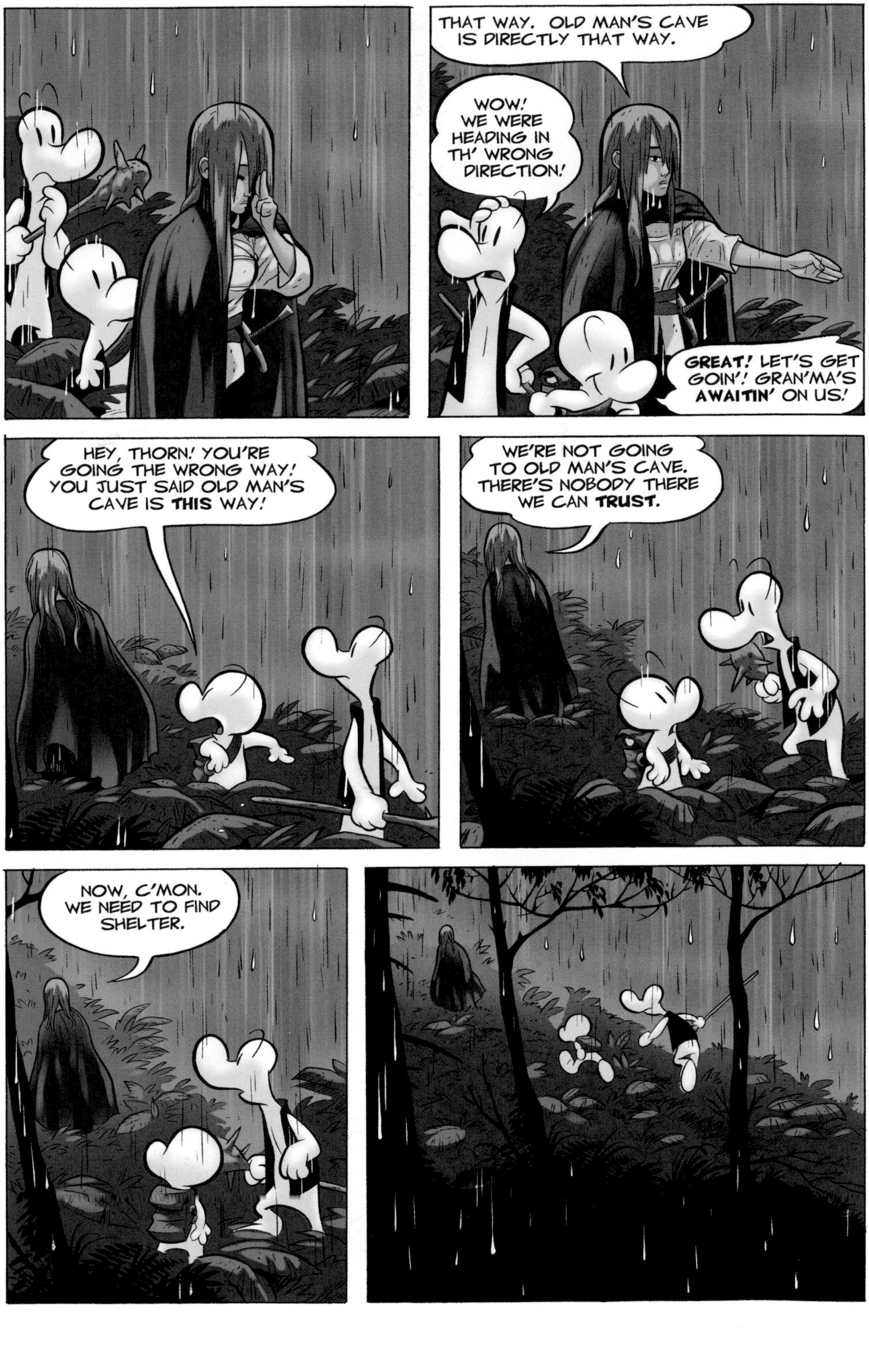
THAT WAY. OLD MAN'S CAVE IS DIRECTLY THAT WAY.
WOW! WE WERE HEADING IN TH' WRONG DIRECTION!
GREAT! LET'S GET GOIN'! GRAN'MA'S **AWAITIN'** ON US!
HEY, THORN! YOU'RE GOING THE WRONG WAY! YOU JUST SAID OLD MAN'S CAVE IS **THIS** WAY!
WE'RE NOT GOING TO OLD MAN'S CAVE. THERE'S NOBODY THERE WE CAN **TRUST.**
NOW, C'MON. WE NEED TO FIND SHELTER.

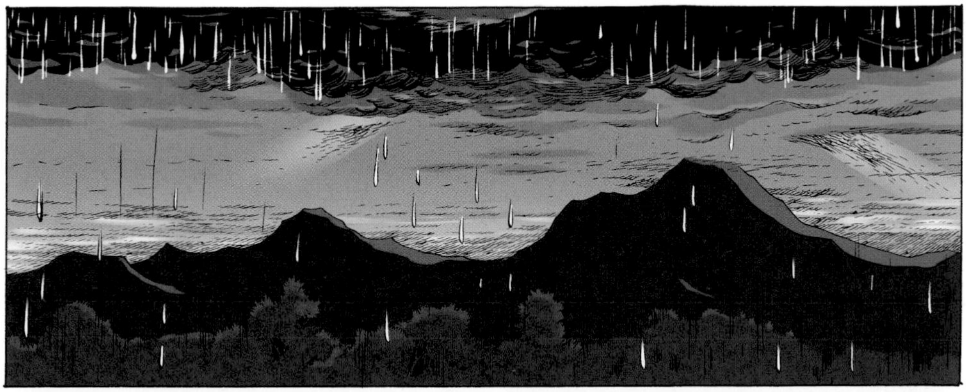

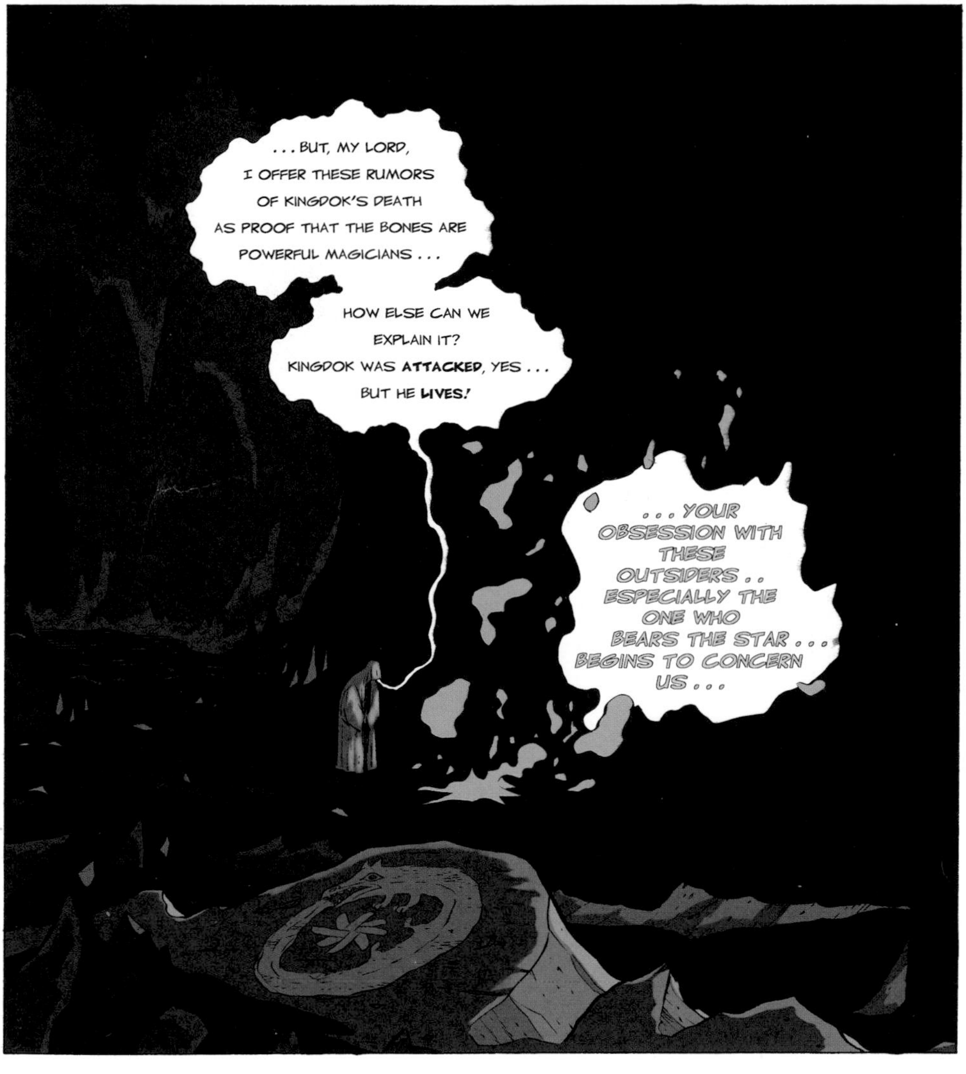

. . . BUT, MY LORD, I OFFER THESE RUMORS OF KINGDOK'S DEATH AS PROOF THAT THE BONES ARE POWERFUL MAGICIANS . . .
HOW ELSE CAN WE EXPLAIN IT? KINGDOK WAS **ATTACKED**, YES . . . BUT HE **LIVES!**
. . . YOUR OBSESSION WITH THESE OUTSIDERS . . ESPECIALLY THE ONE WHO BEARS THE STAR . . . BEGINS TO CONCERN US . . .

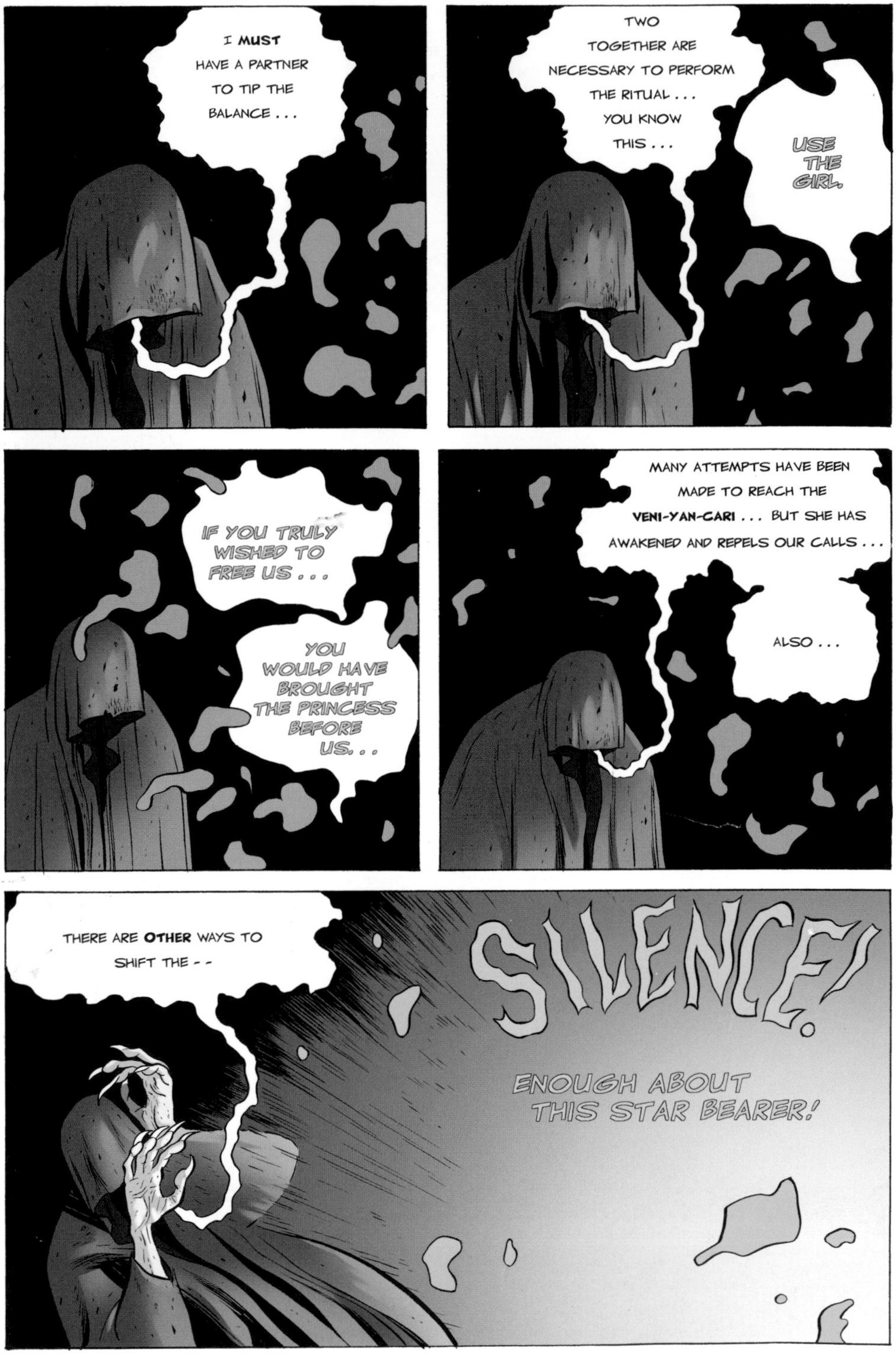
I **MUST** HAVE A PARTNER TO TIP THE BALANCE . . .
TWO TOGETHER ARE NECESSARY TO PERFORM THE RITUAL . . . YOU KNOW THIS . . .
USE THE GIRL.
IF YOU TRULY WISHED TO FREE US . . .
YOU WOULD HAVE BROUGHT THE PRINCESS BEFORE US. . .
MANY ATTEMPTS HAVE BEEN MADE TO REACH THE **VENI-YAN-CARI** . . . BUT SHE HAS AWAKENED AND REPELS OUR CALLS . . .
ALSO . . .
THERE ARE **OTHER** WAYS TO SHIFT THE - -
SILENCE!
ENOUGH ABOUT THIS STAR BEARER!

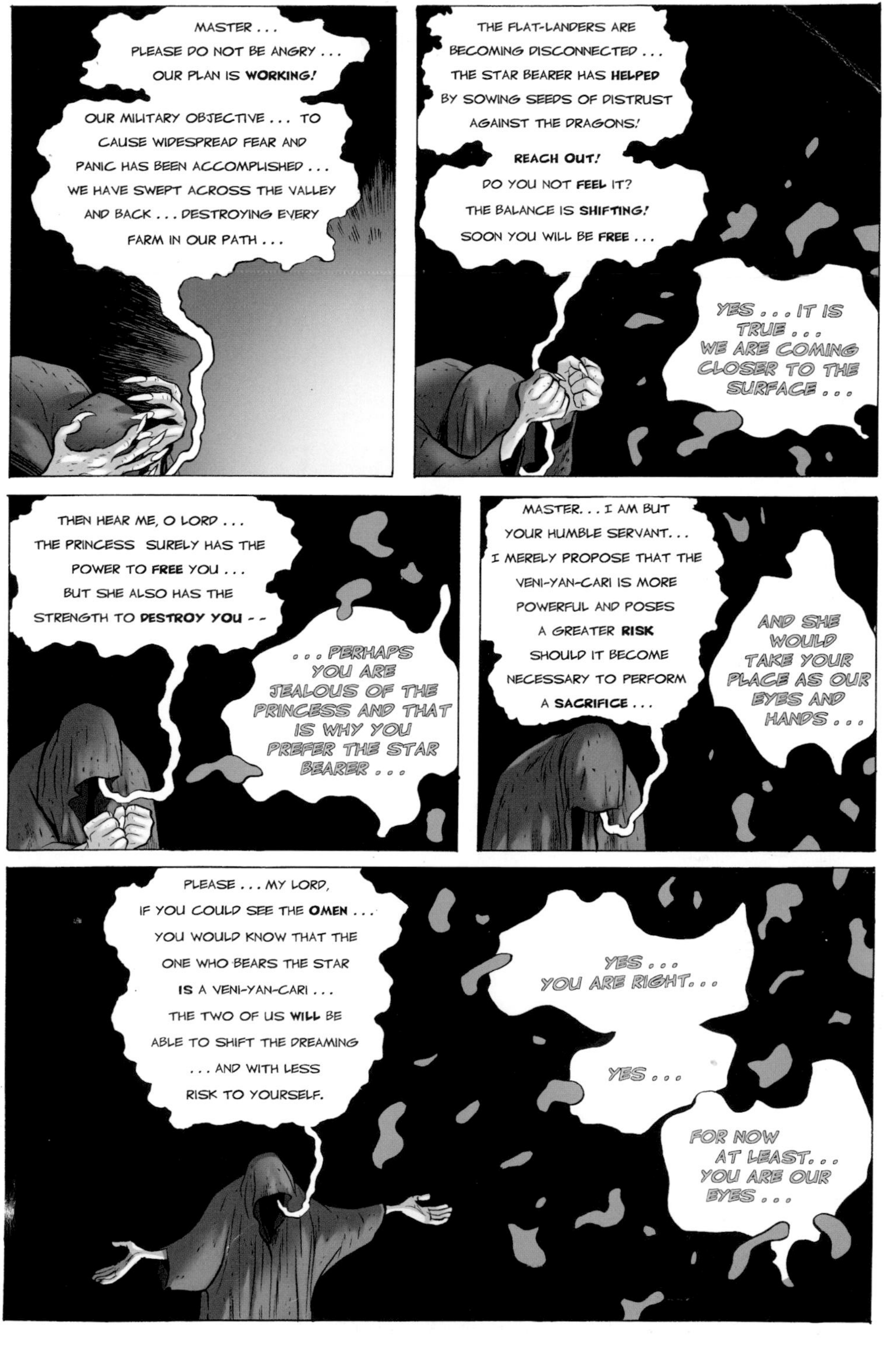
MASTER . . .
PLEASE DO NOT BE ANGRY . . .
OUR PLAN IS WORKING!
OUR MILITARY OBJECTIVE . . . TO CAUSE WIDESPREAD FEAR AND PANIC HAS BEEN ACCOMPLISHED . . . WE HAVE SWEPT ACROSS THE VALLEY AND BACK . . . DESTROYING EVERY FARM IN OUR PATH . . .
THE FLAT-LANDERS ARE BECOMING DISCONNECTED . . . THE STAR BEARER HAS HELPED BY SOWING SEEDS OF DISTRUST AGAINST THE DRAGONS!
REACH OUT! DO YOU NOT FEEL IT? THE BALANCE IS SHIFTING! SOON YOU WILL BE FREE . . .
YES . . . IT IS TRUE . . . WE ARE COMING CLOSER TO THE SURFACE . . .
THEN HEAR ME, O LORD . . . THE PRINCESS SURELY HAS THE POWER TO FREE YOU . . . BUT SHE ALSO HAS THE STRENGTH TO DESTROY YOU - -
. . . PERHAPS YOU ARE JEALOUS OF THE PRINCESS AND THAT IS WHY YOU PREFER THE STAR BEARER . . .
MASTER. . . I AM BUT YOUR HUMBLE SERVANT. . . I MERELY PROPOSE THAT THE VENI-YAN-CARI IS MORE POWERFUL AND POSES A GREATER RISK SHOULD IT BECOME NECESSARY TO PERFORM A SACRIFICE . . .
AND SHE WOULD TAKE YOUR PLACE AS OUR EYES AND HANDS . . .
PLEASE . . . MY LORD, IF YOU COULD SEE THE OMEN . . . YOU WOULD KNOW THAT THE ONE WHO BEARS THE STAR IS A VENI-YAN-CARI . . . THE TWO OF US WILL BE ABLE TO SHIFT THE DREAMING . . . AND WITH LESS RISK TO YOURSELF.
YES . . . YOU ARE RIGHT. . .
YES . . .
FOR NOW AT LEAST. . . YOU ARE OUR EYES . . .

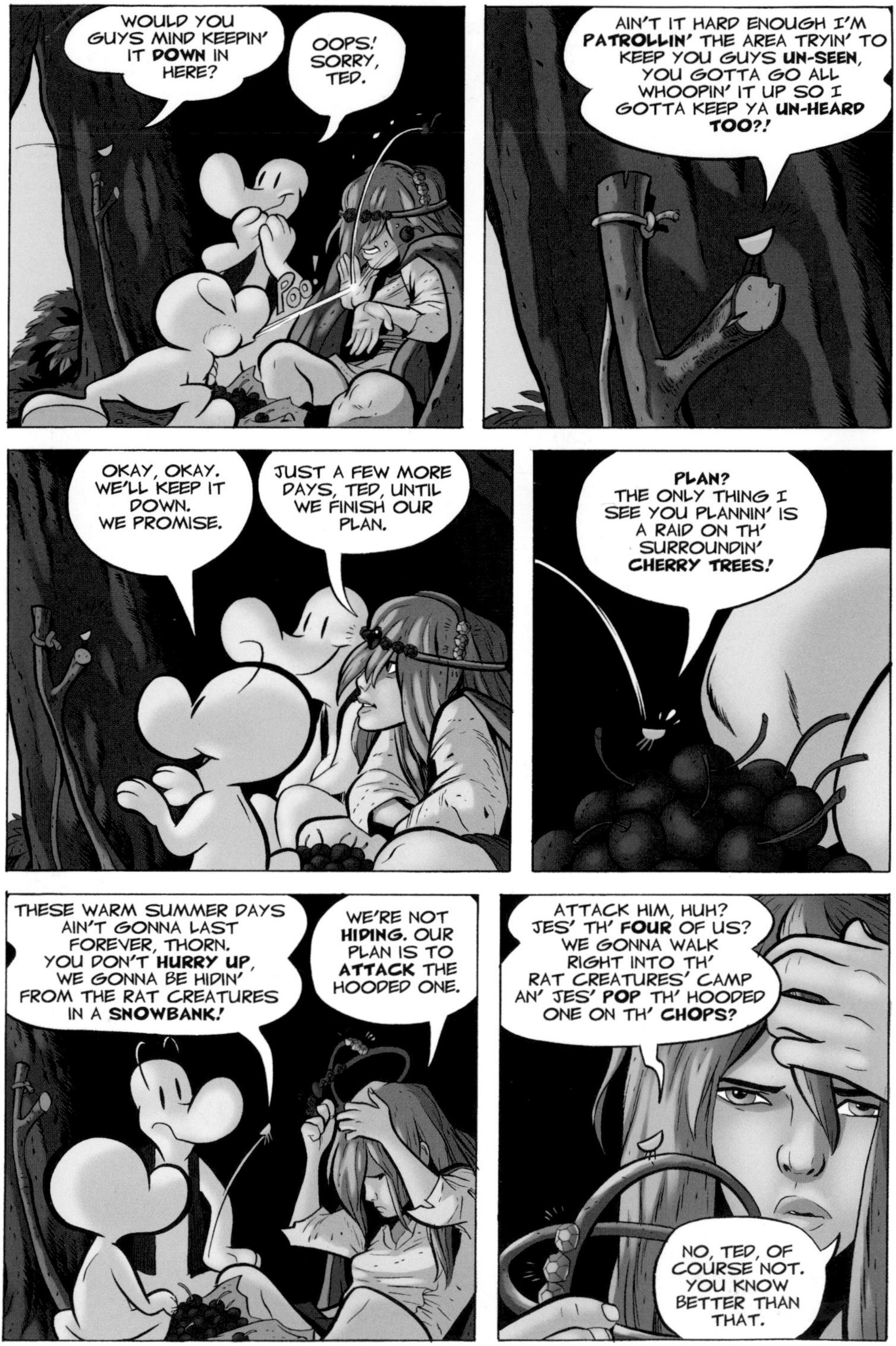
WOULD YOU GUYS MIND KEEPIN' IT **DOWN** IN HERE?
OOPS! SORRY, TED.
POO!
AIN'T IT HARD ENOUGH I'M **PATROLLIN'** THE AREA TRYIN' TO KEEP YOU GUYS **UN-SEEN**, YOU GOTTA GO ALL WHOOPIN' IT UP SO I GOTTA KEEP YA **UN-HEARD TOO?!**
OKAY, OKAY. WE'LL KEEP IT DOWN. WE PROMISE.
JUST A FEW MORE DAYS, TED, UNTIL WE FINISH OUR PLAN.
PLAN? THE ONLY THING I SEE YOU PLANNIN' IS A RAID ON TH' SURROUNDIN' **CHERRY TREES!**
THESE WARM SUMMER DAYS AIN'T GONNA LAST FOREVER, THORN. YOU DON'T **HURRY UP**, WE GONNA BE HIDIN' FROM THE RAT CREATURES IN A **SNOWBANK!**
WE'RE NOT **HIDING.** OUR PLAN IS TO **ATTACK** THE HOODED ONE.
ATTACK HIM, HUH? JES' TH' **FOUR** OF US? WE GONNA WALK RIGHT INTO TH' RAT CREATURES' CAMP AN' JES' **POP** TH' HOODED ONE ON TH' **CHOPS?**
NO, TED, OF COURSE NOT. YOU KNOW BETTER THAN THAT.

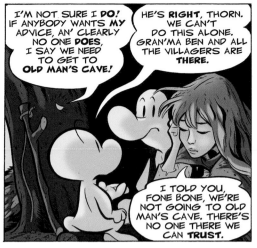

I'M NOT SURE I **DO!** IF ANYBODY WANTS **MY** ADVICE, AN' CLEARLY NO ONE **DOES,** I SAY WE NEED TO GET TO **OLD MAN'S CAVE!**

HE'S **RIGHT,** THORN. WE CAN'T DO THIS ALONE. GRAN'MA BEN AND ALL THE VILLAGERS ARE **THERE.**

I TOLD YOU, FONE BONE, WE'RE NOT GOING TO OLD MAN'S CAVE. THERE'S NO ONE THERE WE CAN **TRUST.**

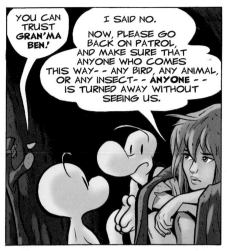

YOU CAN TRUST **GRAN'MA BEN!**

I SAID NO. NOW, PLEASE GO BACK ON PATROL, AND MAKE SURE THAT ANYONE WHO COMES THIS WAY-- ANY BIRD, ANY ANIMAL, OR ANY INSECT-- **ANYONE** -- IS TURNED AWAY WITHOUT SEEING US.

ALL RIGHT, I'M **GOIN'.** BUT WHEN THIS IS ALL OVER, GRAN'MA BEN GONNA SQUISH ME LIKE A **BUG** FOR DISOBEYIN' HER.

ARE YOU **SURE** ABOUT GRAN'MA BEN? 'CAUSE TO TELL TH' **TRUTH,** I KINDA **MISS** HER.

EXCUSE ME. . . I'M GOING TO FIX SOME SUPPER. WOULD YOU MIND HANDING ME SOME OF THAT FUEL, SMILEY?

YEAH, OKAY. . .

IT'S JUST THAT MAYBE I DON'T UNDERSTAND TH' **PLAN.**

COULD YOU MAKE A LITTLE PILE WITH THOSE DROPPINGS?

DROPPINGS? EEYUU!

DRIED ANIMAL DROPPINGS.

MAKES A SMOKELESS FIRE.

WE CAN WORK ON OUR PLAN WHILE WE EAT.

THORN, WE DON'T **HAVE** A PLAN.

YEAH, HOW ARE WE GONNA **GET** THE HOODED ONE? WE DON'T KNOW NOTHIN' **ABOUT** HIM EXCEPT THAT HE APPEARS IN YOUR **DREAMS.**

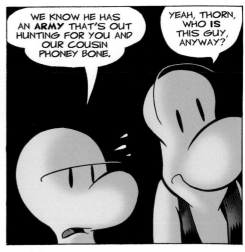

WE KNOW HE HAS AN **ARMY** THAT'S OUT HUNTING FOR YOU AND OUR COUSIN PHONEY BONE.

YEAH, THORN, WHO **IS** THIS GUY, ANYWAY?

I DON'T KNOW. THERE'S A PROTECTIVE SPELL AROUND THE HOODED ONE SIMILAR TO THE ONE TED AND I PUT AROUND THE FOUR OF **US.**

. . . BUT I DO KNOW **SOME** THINGS.

I KNOW THE HOODED ONE DRAWS HIS POWER FROM A DREAM BEING CALLED THE **LORD OF THE LOCUSTS.**

THESE POWERS LET THE HOODED ONE TRAVEL IN - -AND IN SOME CASES EVEN **PERVERT** - - OTHER PEOPLE'S DREAMS.

THE MORE FEAR HE CAUSES, THE MORE POWERFUL HE BECOMES!

SO WHY'S HE WANT YOU AN' PHONEY?

I **BELIEVE** HE WANTS US BOTH FOR THE SAME PURPOSE . . . TO SPEED THE RELEASE OF HIS **MASTER,** THE LORD OF THE LOCUSTS, WHO IS TRAPPED IN **STONE.**

THE HOODED ONE THINKS YOUR COUSIN AND I HAVE THE POWER TO HELP FREE HIM.

WHOA, WAIT A MINUTE. I DON'T GET IT . . . **YOU** HAVE A POWER, SO **YOU** MIGHT BE USEFUL, BUT **PHONEY** DOESN'T.' WHAT'S SO SPECIAL ABOUT PHONEY?

BESIDES HOW LOUD HE IS.'

WELL, DURING THE COW RACE HE TURNED THE TOWNSPEOPLE AGAINST GRAN'MA BEN . . .

THEN HE RILED UP FEAR AND ANGER AT THE **DRAGONS** FOR HIS DRAGONSLAYER SCAM.'

THAT'S **EXACTLY** THE KIND OF THING THAT FEEDS THE HOODED ONE'S POWERS.

WE KNOW HE CAUSES TROUBLE, BUT --

BOY, DO WE KNOW.'

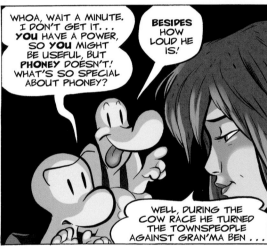

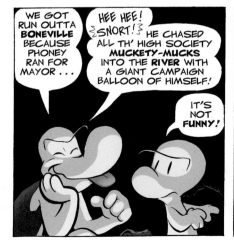

WE GOT RUN OUTTA **BONEVILLE** BECAUSE PHONEY RAN FOR MAYOR . . .

HEE HEE! ¿SNORT!¿ HE CHASED ALL TH' HIGH SOCIETY **MUCKETY-MUCKS** INTO THE **RIVER** WITH A GIANT CAMPAIGN BALLOON OF HIMSELF!

IT'S NOT **FUNNY!**

IT WAS SORTA FUNNY WHEN THE ANGRY MOB ATE A BUNCH OF PHONEY'S ROTTEN **PRUNE TARTS,** AN' HAD TO LEAVE IN A HURRY!

MY **POINT** IS THAT PHONEY WOULD NEVER DO ANYTHING TO HELP THE HOODED ONE **ON PURPOSE!**

I BELIEVE THAT. I DO . . .

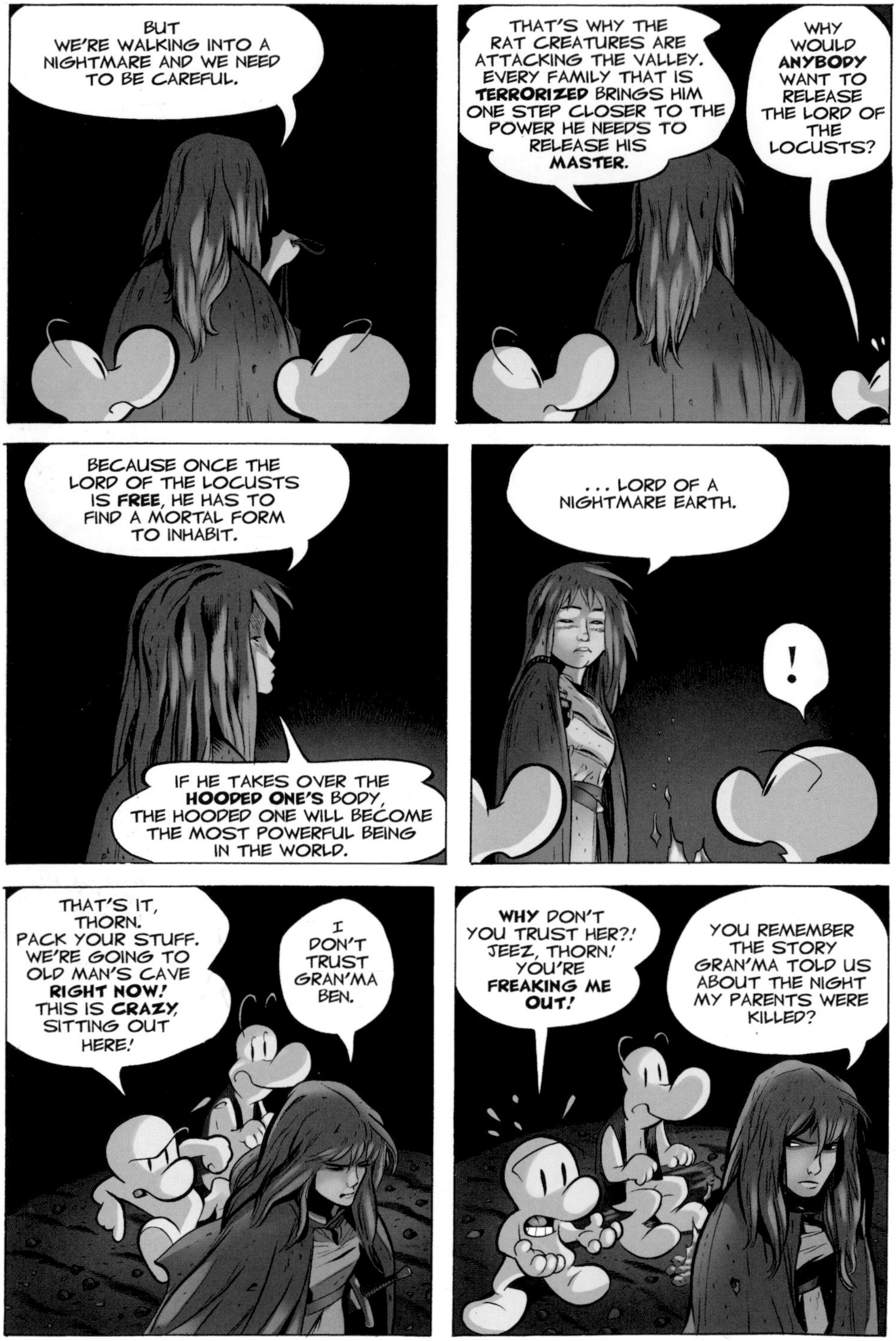
BUT WE'RE WALKING INTO A NIGHTMARE AND WE NEED TO BE CAREFUL.
THAT'S WHY THE RAT CREATURES ARE ATTACKING THE VALLEY. EVERY FAMILY THAT IS **TERRORIZED** BRINGS HIM ONE STEP CLOSER TO THE POWER HE NEEDS TO RELEASE HIS **MASTER.**
WHY WOULD **ANYBODY** WANT TO RELEASE THE LORD OF THE LOCUSTS?
BECAUSE ONCE THE LORD OF THE LOCUSTS IS **FREE**, HE HAS TO FIND A MORTAL FORM TO INHABIT.
IF HE TAKES OVER THE **HOODED ONE'S** BODY, THE HOODED ONE WILL BECOME THE MOST POWERFUL BEING IN THE WORLD.
. . . LORD OF A NIGHTMARE EARTH.
!
THAT'S IT, THORN. PACK YOUR STUFF. WE'RE GOING TO OLD MAN'S CAVE **RIGHT NOW!** THIS IS **CRAZY**, SITTING OUT HERE!
I DON'T TRUST GRAN'MA BEN.
WHY DON'T YOU TRUST HER?! JEEZ, THORN! YOU'RE **FREAKING ME OUT!**
YOU REMEMBER THE STORY GRAN'MA TOLD US ABOUT THE NIGHT MY PARENTS WERE KILLED?

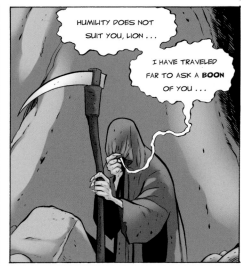

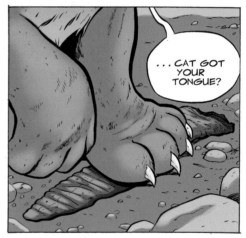

PROTECTION SPELL

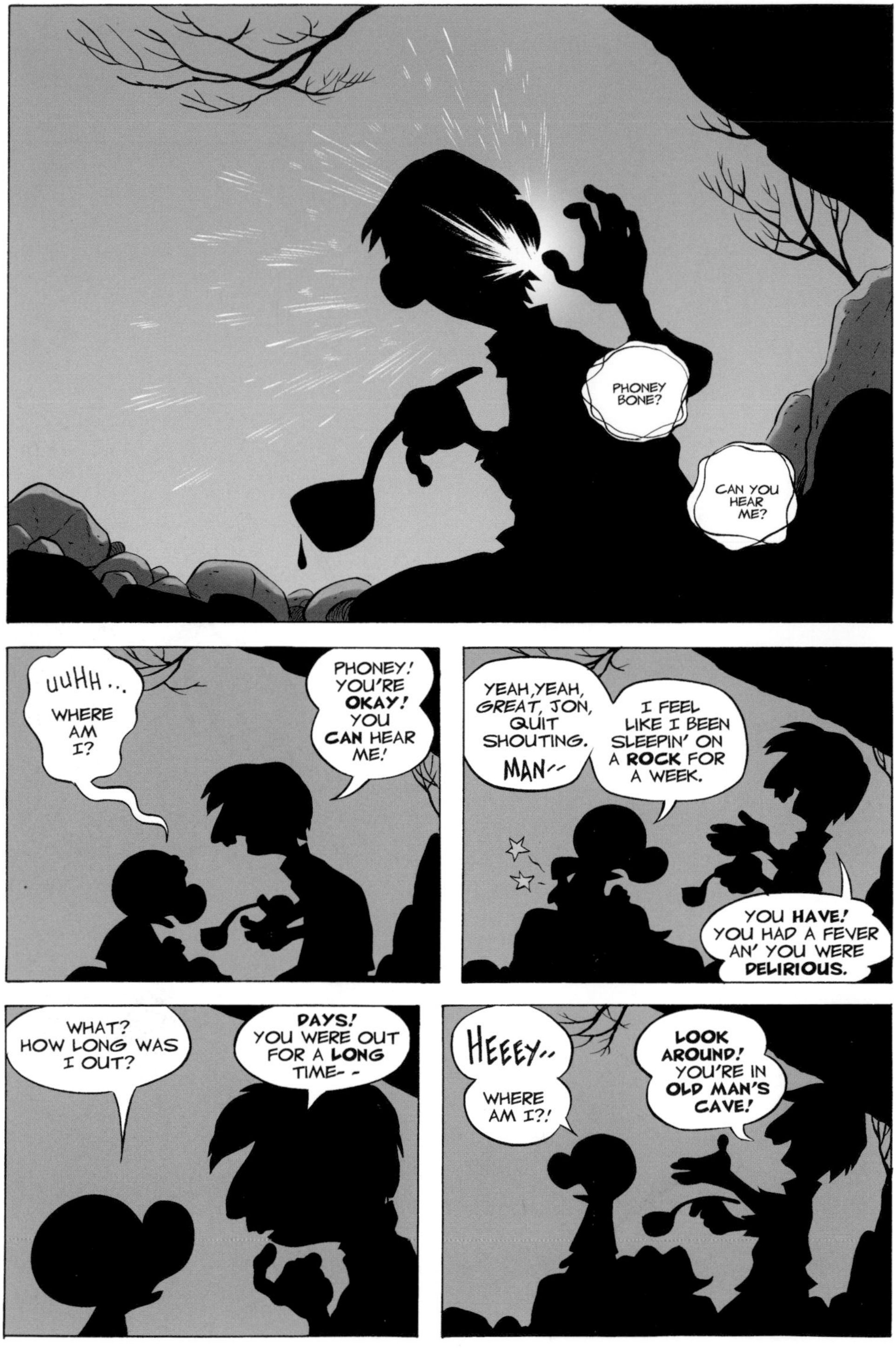
PHONEY BONE?
CAN YOU HEAR ME?
UUHH... WHERE AM I?
PHONEY! YOU'RE **OKAY!** YOU **CAN** HEAR ME!
YEAH, YEAH, *GREAT*, JON, QUIT SHOUTING.
MAN--
I FEEL LIKE I BEEN SLEEPIN' ON A **ROCK** FOR A WEEK.
YOU **HAVE!** YOU HAD A FEVER AN' YOU WERE **DELIRIOUS.**
WHAT? HOW LONG WAS I OUT?
DAYS! YOU WERE OUT FOR A **LONG** TIME--
HEEEY.. WHERE AM I?!
LOOK AROUND! YOU'RE IN **OLD MAN'S CAVE!**

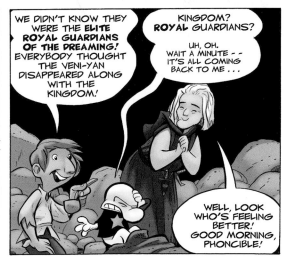

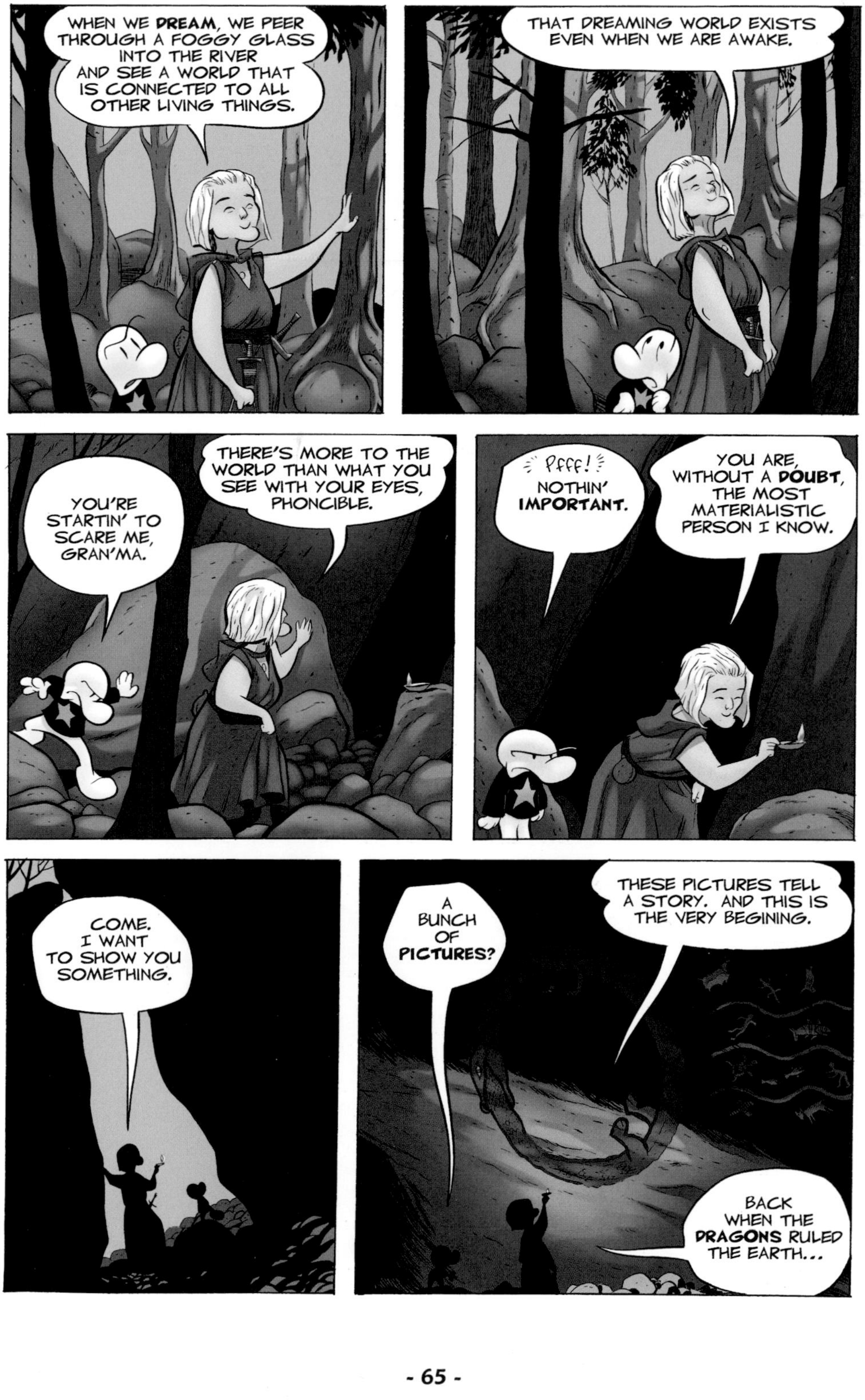
WHEN WE DREAM, WE PEER THROUGH A FOGGY GLASS INTO THE RIVER AND SEE A WORLD THAT IS CONNECTED TO ALL OTHER LIVING THINGS.
THAT DREAMING WORLD EXISTS EVEN WHEN WE ARE AWAKE.
YOU'RE STARTIN' TO SCARE ME, GRAN'MA.
THERE'S MORE TO THE WORLD THAN WHAT YOU SEE WITH YOUR EYES, PHONCIBLE.
Pfff! NOTHIN' IMPORTANT.
YOU ARE, WITHOUT A DOUBT, THE MOST MATERIALISTIC PERSON I KNOW.
COME. I WANT TO SHOW YOU SOMETHING.
A BUNCH OF PICTURES?
THESE PICTURES TELL A STORY. AND THIS IS THE VERY BEGINING.
BACK WHEN THE DRAGONS RULED THE EARTH...

WHEN THE WORLD WAS VERY, VERY NEW, THE **FIRST** DRAGON WAS A QUEEN NAMED **MIM.** MIM MAINTAINED THE DREAMING BY WATCHING ITS FLOW AND KEEPING IT **BALANCED.**

THE **DREAMING** IS A THING OF GREAT DELICACY, AND BALANCE IS MOST IMPORTANT.

MIM WATCHED THE DREAMING WITH **CARE,** AND ALL CREATURES LIVED TOGETHER IN PEACE AND HARMONY...

...UNTIL ONE DAY A SPIRIT KNOWN AS THE **LORD OF THE LOCUSTS** BECAME UNHAPPY.

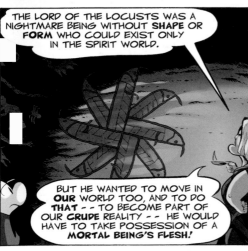

THE LORD OF THE LOCUSTS WAS A NIGHTMARE BEING WITHOUT **SHAPE** OR **FORM** WHO COULD EXIST ONLY IN THE SPIRIT WORLD.

BUT HE WANTED TO MOVE IN **OUR** WORLD TOO, AND TO DO **THAT** - - TO BECOME PART OF OUR **CRUDE** REALITY - - HE WOULD HAVE TO TAKE POSSESSION OF A **MORTAL BEING'S FLESH!**

HE CHOSE MIM, **QUEEN OF THE DRAGONS,** THE MOST POWERFUL DREAMER IN THE WORLD.

DRAGONS AREN'T **IMMORTAL?**

DRAGONS LIVE FOR A VERY LONG TIME, BUT THEY ARE MORTAL. EVERYTHING IN **OUR** WORLD IS MORTAL.

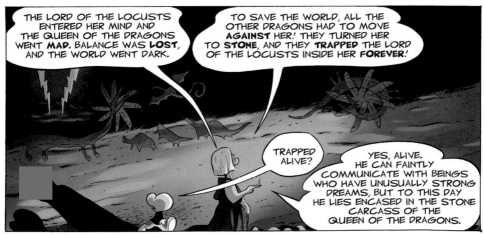

THE LORD OF THE LOCUSTS ENTERED HER MIND AND THE QUEEN OF THE DRAGONS WENT **MAD.** BALANCE WAS **LOST,** AND THE WORLD WENT DARK.

TO SAVE THE WORLD, ALL THE OTHER DRAGONS HAD TO MOVE **AGAINST** HER! THEY TURNED HER TO **STONE,** AND THEY **TRAPPED** THE LORD OF THE LOCUSTS INSIDE HER **FOREVER!**

TRAPPED ALIVE?

YES, ALIVE. HE CAN FAINTLY COMMUNICATE WITH BEINGS WHO HAVE UNUSUALLY STRONG DREAMS, BUT TO THIS DAY HE LIES ENCASED IN THE STONE CARCASS OF THE QUEEN OF THE DRAGONS.

AFTER THE FRIGHT CAUSED BY THEIR QUEEN, THE HIGH COUNCIL OF DRAGONS NO LONGER FELT THEY SHOULD BE THE SOLE GUARDIANS OF THE DREAMING...

SO THEY BEGAN TO SEARCH FOR A **HUMAN** THEY COULD TRUST, AND THEY FOUND A YOUNG GIRL NAMED **VEN.**

SHE WAS **VEN HARVESTAR,** THE FIRST QUEEN OF THE HUMANS. SHE WAS **MY** ANCESTOR, AND THORN'S ANCESTOR.

THESE COINS WERE FORGED BY THE DRAGONS AS A TOKEN OF THE COVENANT BETWEEN OUR TWO RACES TO UPHOLD AND MAINTAIN THE BALANCE OF THE **DREAMING...**

YEAH, YEAH, REAL NICE. LET'S SKIP **AHEAD** A FEW GENERATIONS. WHAT'S THIS GOT TO DO WITH **ME?**

A GREAT DEAL.

SOMEONE WANTS TO **FREE** THE LORD OF THE LOCUSTS...

WHAT?

...AND THEY NEED **YOU** TO DO IT.

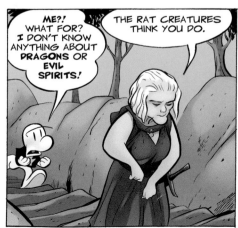

ME?! WHAT FOR? I DON'T KNOW ANYTHING ABOUT **DRAGONS** OR **EVIL SPIRITS!**

THE RAT CREATURES THINK YOU DO.

IT'S A **SETUP!** I'M BEING **FRAMED!**

THE BEST INFORMATION WE HAVE IS THAT THE RAT CREATURES AND A **ROGUE** VENI-YAN WARRIOR CALLED **THE HOODED ONE** ARE SEARCHING FOR YOU IN ORDER TO FREE THE ANCIENT LORD OF THE LOCUSTS.

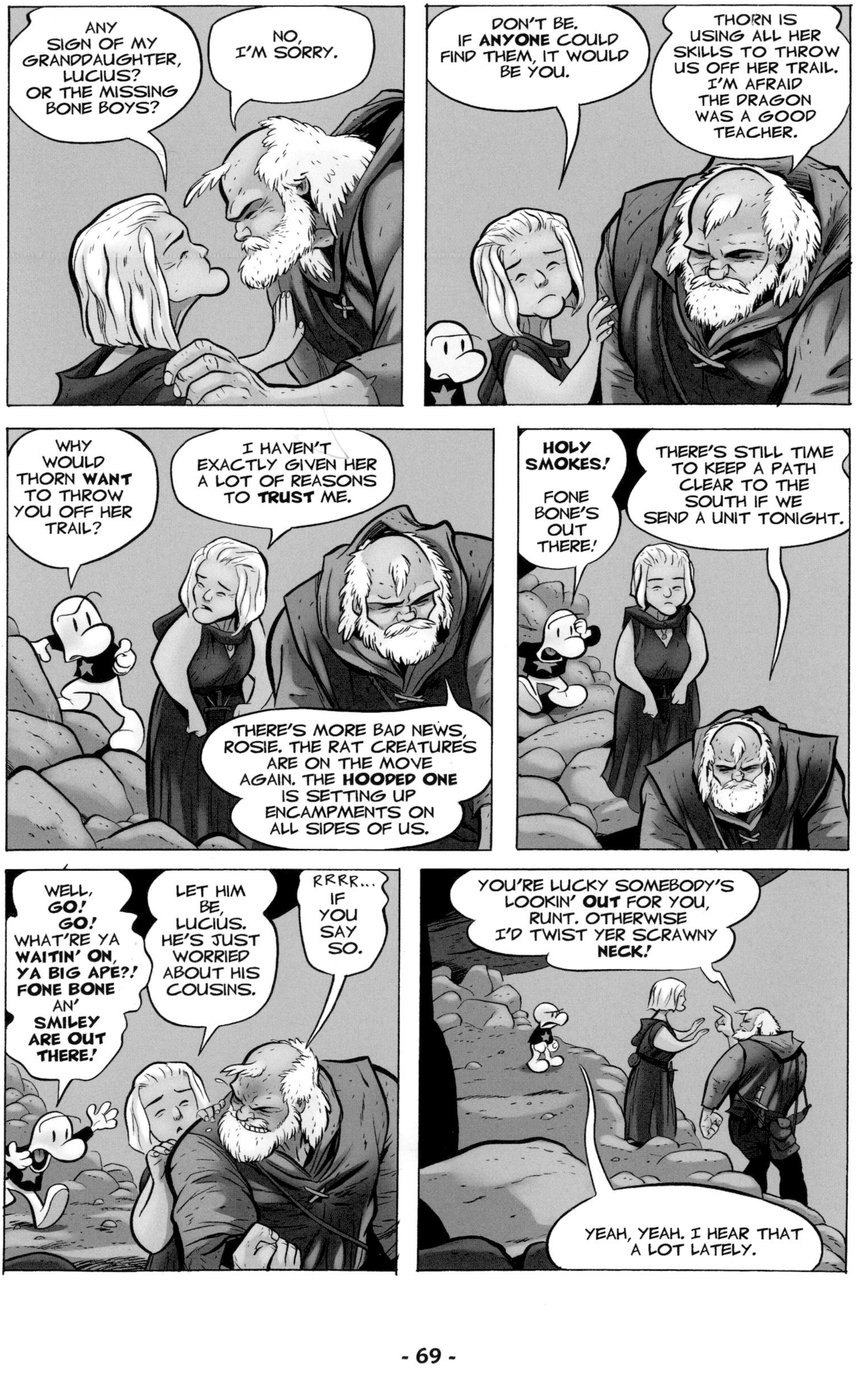
ANY SIGN OF MY GRANDDAUGHTER, LUCIUS? OR THE MISSING BONE BOYS?
NO, I'M SORRY.
DON'T BE. IF ANYONE COULD FIND THEM, IT WOULD BE YOU.
THORN IS USING ALL HER SKILLS TO THROW US OFF HER TRAIL. I'M AFRAID THE DRAGON WAS A GOOD TEACHER.
WHY WOULD THORN WANT TO THROW YOU OFF HER TRAIL?
I HAVEN'T EXACTLY GIVEN HER A LOT OF REASONS TO TRUST ME.
THERE'S MORE BAD NEWS, ROSIE. THE RAT CREATURES ARE ON THE MOVE AGAIN. THE HOODED ONE IS SETTING UP ENCAMPMENTS ON ALL SIDES OF US.
HOLY SMOKES!
FONE BONE'S OUT THERE!
THERE'S STILL TIME TO KEEP A PATH CLEAR TO THE SOUTH IF WE SEND A UNIT TONIGHT.
WELL, GO! GO! WHAT'RE YA WAITIN' ON, YA BIG APE?! FONE BONE AN' SMILEY ARE OUT THERE!
LET HIM BE, LUCIUS. HE'S JUST WORRIED ABOUT HIS COUSINS.
RRRR... IF YOU SAY SO.
YOU'RE LUCKY SOMEBODY'S LOOKIN' OUT FOR YOU, RUNT. OTHERWISE I'D TWIST YER SCRAWNY NECK!
YEAH, YEAH. I HEAR THAT A LOT LATELY.

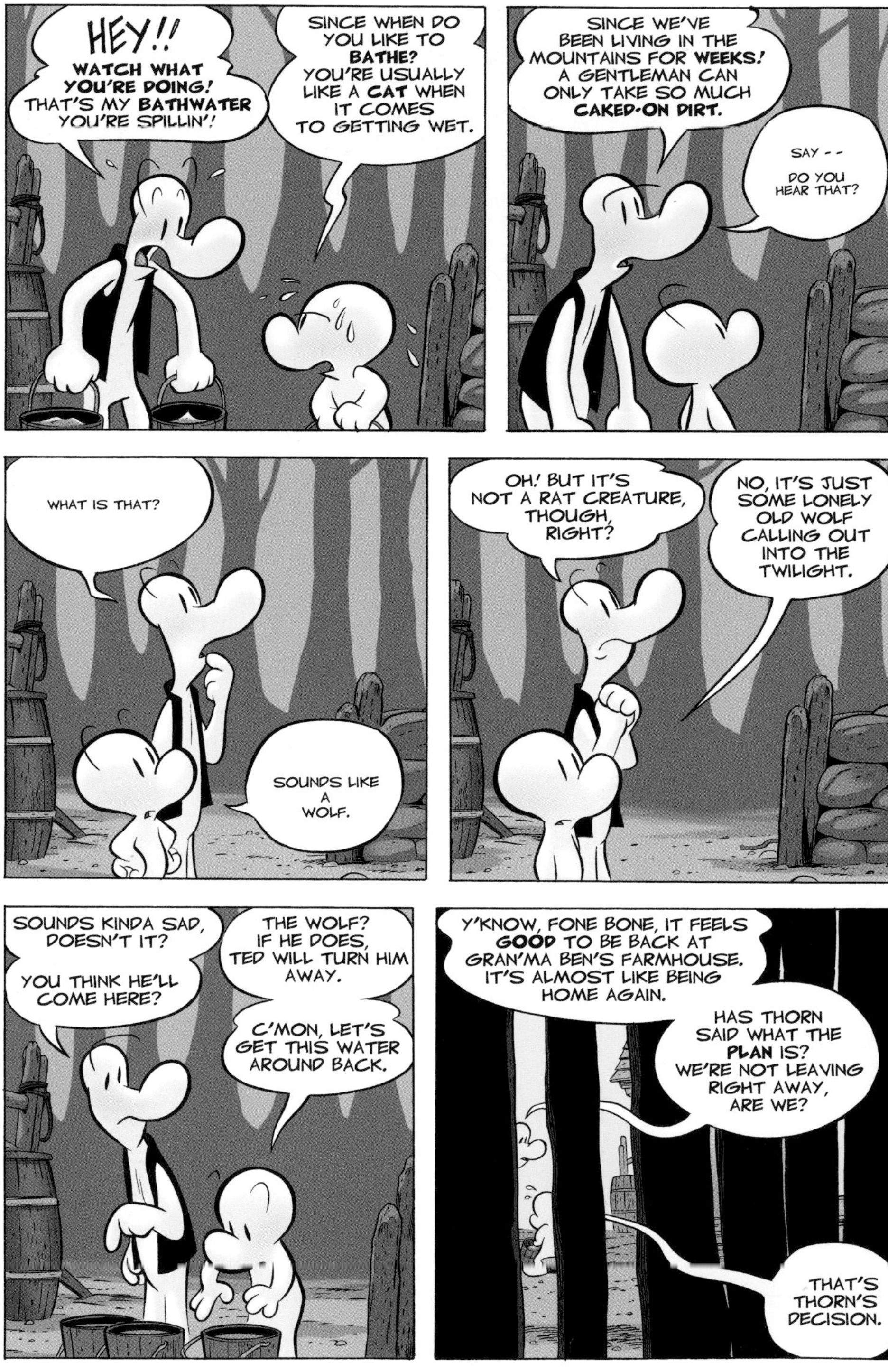
HEY!! WATCH WHAT YOU'RE DOING! THAT'S MY BATHWATER YOU'RE SPILLIN'!
SINCE WHEN DO YOU LIKE TO BATHE? YOU'RE USUALLY LIKE A CAT WHEN IT COMES TO GETTING WET.
SINCE WE'VE BEEN LIVING IN THE MOUNTAINS FOR WEEKS! A GENTLEMAN CAN ONLY TAKE SO MUCH CAKED-ON DIRT.
SAY - - DO YOU HEAR THAT?
WHAT IS THAT?
SOUNDS LIKE A WOLF.
OH! BUT IT'S NOT A RAT CREATURE, THOUGH, RIGHT?
NO, IT'S JUST SOME LONELY OLD WOLF CALLING OUT INTO THE TWILIGHT.
SOUNDS KINDA SAD, DOESN'T IT?
YOU THINK HE'LL COME HERE?
THE WOLF? IF HE DOES, TED WILL TURN HIM AWAY.
C'MON, LET'S GET THIS WATER AROUND BACK.
Y'KNOW, FONE BONE, IT FEELS GOOD TO BE BACK AT GRAN'MA BEN'S FARMHOUSE. IT'S ALMOST LIKE BEING HOME AGAIN.
HAS THORN SAID WHAT THE PLAN IS? WE'RE NOT LEAVING RIGHT AWAY, ARE WE?
THAT'S THORN'S DECISION.

WELL, WHAT DOES SHE **WANT**? ARE WE GONNA STAY HERE, OR ARE WE GONNA GO TO OLD MAN'S CAVE?

I DON'T THINK SHE WANTS TO DO **EITHER**. SHE JUST WANTS TO GET SOME THINGS AND GO BACK TO THE MOUNTAINS.

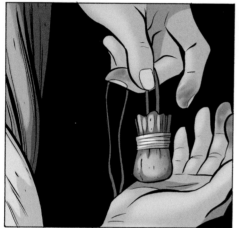

IT'S GRAN'MA BEN, ISN'T IT? THORN DOESN'T TRUST HER ANYMORE.

NOPE. SHE DOESN'T TRUST HER.

WELL, I THINK THORN'S WRONG. I THINK WE **CAN** TRUST GRAN'MA BEN, AND WE SHOULD GO MEET HER AT OLD MAN'S CAVE, LIKE TED WANTS US TO!

SO DO I . . .

. . . BUT UNTIL THORN CHANGES HER MIND, WE'LL JUST HAVE TO BE PATIENT.

AT LEAST UNTIL WE HEAR THIS BIG **PLAN** OF HERS.

YOU THINK SHE REALLY **HAS** A PLAN?

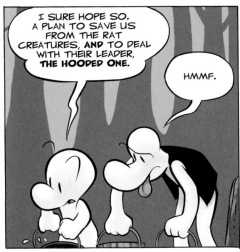

I SURE HOPE SO. A PLAN TO SAVE US FROM THE RAT CREATURES, **AND** TO DEAL WITH THEIR LEADER, **THE HOODED ONE.**

HMMF.

IF THORN **DID** HAVE A PLAN, WHY WOULDN'T SHE TELL IT TO US?

THE PLAN IS TO SNEAK INTO THE RAT CREATURES' ENCAMPMENT AND **ASSASSINATE** THE HOODED ONE . . .

NOW WAIT -- WHOA, WHOA.

WHAT ARE YOU TALKING ABOUT?

YOU THINK AFTER ALL THIS, WE'RE NOT GOING TO BE PART OF THE PLAN?

THIS DOESN'T INVOLVE YOU.

IT'S **MY** PROBLEM.

ALTHOUGH I FEEL I SHOULD **STRESS** THAT IT IS A VERY **STUPID** PLAN.

DOESN'T INVOLVE ME?! THE HOODED ONE IS AFTER **MY** COUSIN PHONEY BONE! "THE ONE WHO BEARS THE STAR," **REMEMBER?**

NOT TO MENTION THAT I'VE BEEN CHASED OFF CLIFFS, PUSHED OFF WATERFALLS, **RAINED ON**, AND BEATEN UP EVERY SINGLE DAY SINCE I **GOT** TO THIS STUPID VALLEY!

WE'RE **IN**, THORN --

YOU'RE NOT MAKING THIS DECISION **WITHOUT** US!

AND BEFORE YOU SAY ANOTHER WORD -- I KNOW YOU'RE MAD AT YOUR GRANDMOTHER FOR LYING ABOUT THE DEATH OF YOUR PARENTS, BUT **MOVE ON.**

SHE THOUGHT SHE WAS PROTECTING YOU.

C'MON, THORN.

LET'S GO TO OLD MAN'S CAVE.

IT'S NOT JUST HER LIES. THERE'S MORE . . .

ALMOST EVERY NIGHT GRAN'MA BEN APPEARS TO ME IN A DREAM . . .

BUT SOMETHING IS WRONG.

SHE SEEMS SPLIT IN TWO . . .

FIRST PULLING ME IN ONE DIRECTION, THEN ANOTHER. IT'S LIKE HAVING TWO DIFFERENT GRAN'MA BENS BATTLING FOR POSSESSION OF ME.

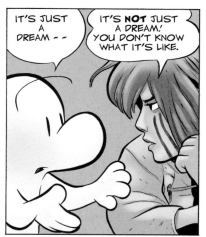

IT'S JUST A DREAM - -

IT'S **NOT** JUST A DREAM! YOU DON'T KNOW WHAT IT'S LIKE.

YOU DON'T KNOW WHAT IT'S LIKE TO NEVER KNOW YOUR MOTHER AND FATHER.

YES, WE DO.

WHAT DID YOU SAY?

WE'RE ORPHANS TOO. ME, AND FONE BONE, AND PHONEY. WE'RE ALL THE FAMILY WE **GOT**.

UNTIL WE CAME HERE, THAT IS. YOU AND GRAN'MA BEN TOOK CARE OF US -- EVEN WHEN IT MEANT YOUR OWN LIVES WOULD BE IN DANGER.

WHEN WE WERE KIDS, PHONEY WAS THE OLDEST AND HE TOOK CARE OF US.

I ALWAYS FIGURED THAT WAS **WHY** HE GOT SO RESOURCEFUL AND STINGY.

WHEN PHONEY PULLS SOME STUPID SCAM THAT MAKES ME **CRAZY**, I KNOW DEEP DOWN HE DOESN'T MEAN TO HURT ANYONE . . . . . . IN **HIS** MIND, HE'S STILL LOOKING OUT FOR US.

DEEP DOWN YOU KNOW IF YOU CAN TRUST SOMEONE.

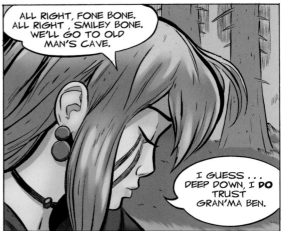

ALL RIGHT, FONE BONE. ALL RIGHT, SMILEY BONE. WE'LL GO TO OLD MAN'S CAVE.

I GUESS . . . DEEP DOWN, I **DO** TRUST GRAN'MA BEN.

GRAB YOUR STUFF, AND LET'S GO.

MAN, I HOPE YOU'RE RIGHT ABOUT THIS!

HEY, **THORN!** CAN I WEAR SOME OF THAT WAR PAINT, TOO? HUH, CAN I?

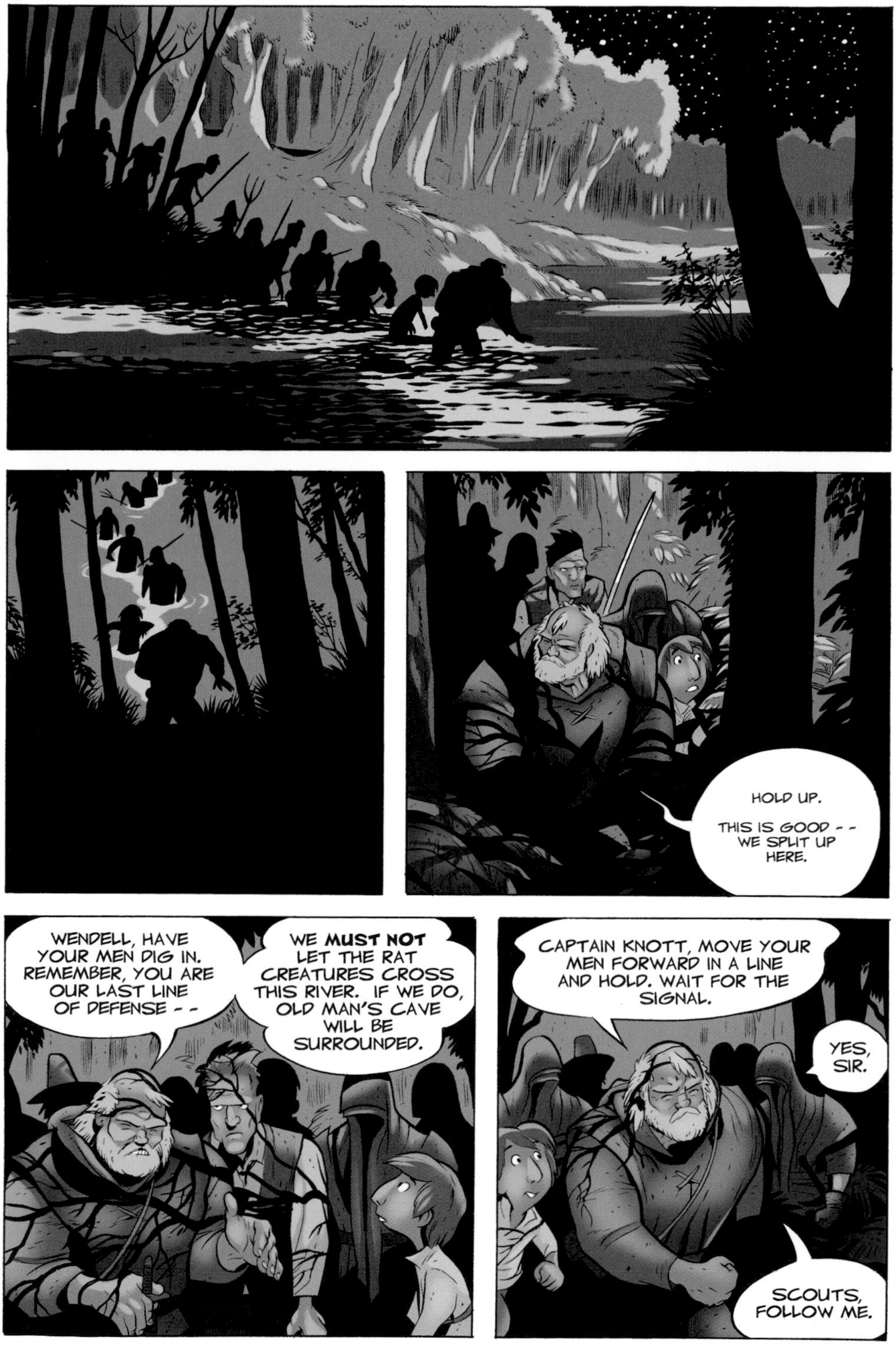
HOLD UP.
THIS IS GOOD - - WE SPLIT UP HERE.
WENDELL, HAVE YOUR MEN DIG IN. REMEMBER, YOU ARE OUR LAST LINE OF DEFENSE - -
WE **MUST NOT** LET THE RAT CREATURES CROSS THIS RIVER. IF WE DO, OLD MAN'S CAVE WILL BE SURROUNDED.
CAPTAIN KNOTT, MOVE YOUR MEN FORWARD IN A LINE AND HOLD. WAIT FOR THE SIGNAL.
YES, SIR.
SCOUTS, FOLLOW ME.

JONATHAN, I WANT YOU TO GO UP THE MIDDLE QUIET AS A GHOST. IF YOU SEE THE ENEMY, SNEAK BACK AND WARN OUR BOYS TO PREPARE THE AMBUSH.

RIGHT.

SON, YOU MOVE UP THE NORTH BANK AND KEEP YOUR EYES PEELED -- OR WHATEVER IT IS YOU DO WITH THAT HOOD PULLED OVER YOUR FACE.

WE ARE WELL TRAINED TO SEE.

VERY GOOD.

NOW, REMEMBER, DO **NOT** ENGAGE THE ENEMY! YOUR JOB IS TO WARN OUR BOYS . . .

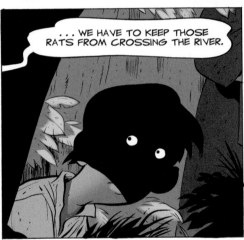

. . . WE HAVE TO KEEP THOSE RATS FROM CROSSING THE RIVER.

LUCIUS . . .

WHO'S THERE?

DO NOT DRAW YOUR WEAPON . . . . .

IT IS ME . . .

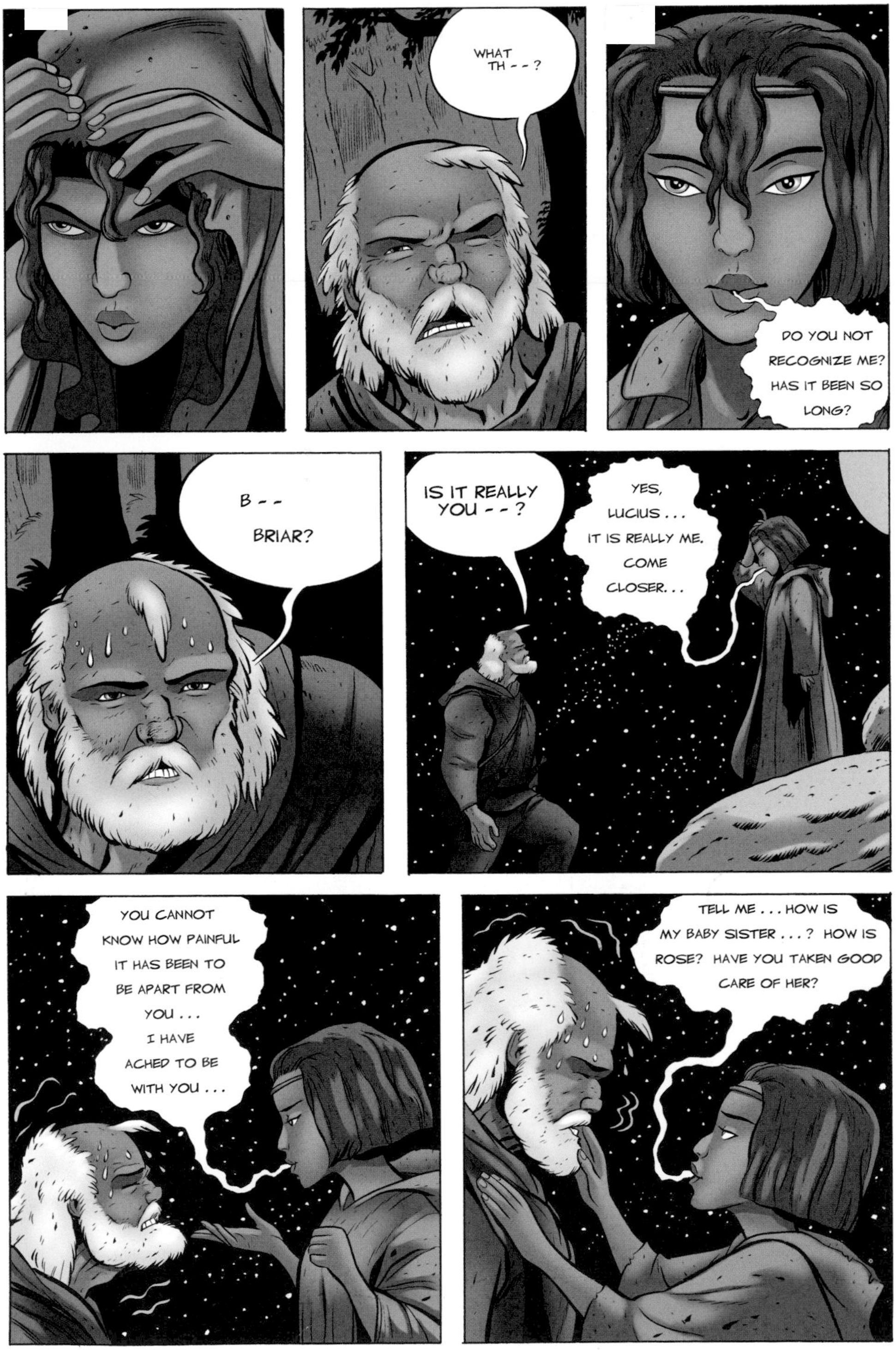
WHAT TH - - ?
DO YOU NOT RECOGNIZE ME? HAS IT BEEN SO LONG?
B - - BRIAR?
IS IT REALLY YOU - - ?
YES, LUCIUS . . . IT IS REALLY ME. COME CLOSER . . .
YOU CANNOT KNOW HOW PAINFUL IT HAS BEEN TO BE APART FROM YOU . . . I HAVE ACHED TO BE WITH YOU . . .
TELL ME . . . HOW IS MY BABY SISTER . . . ? HOW IS ROSE? HAVE YOU TAKEN GOOD CARE OF HER?

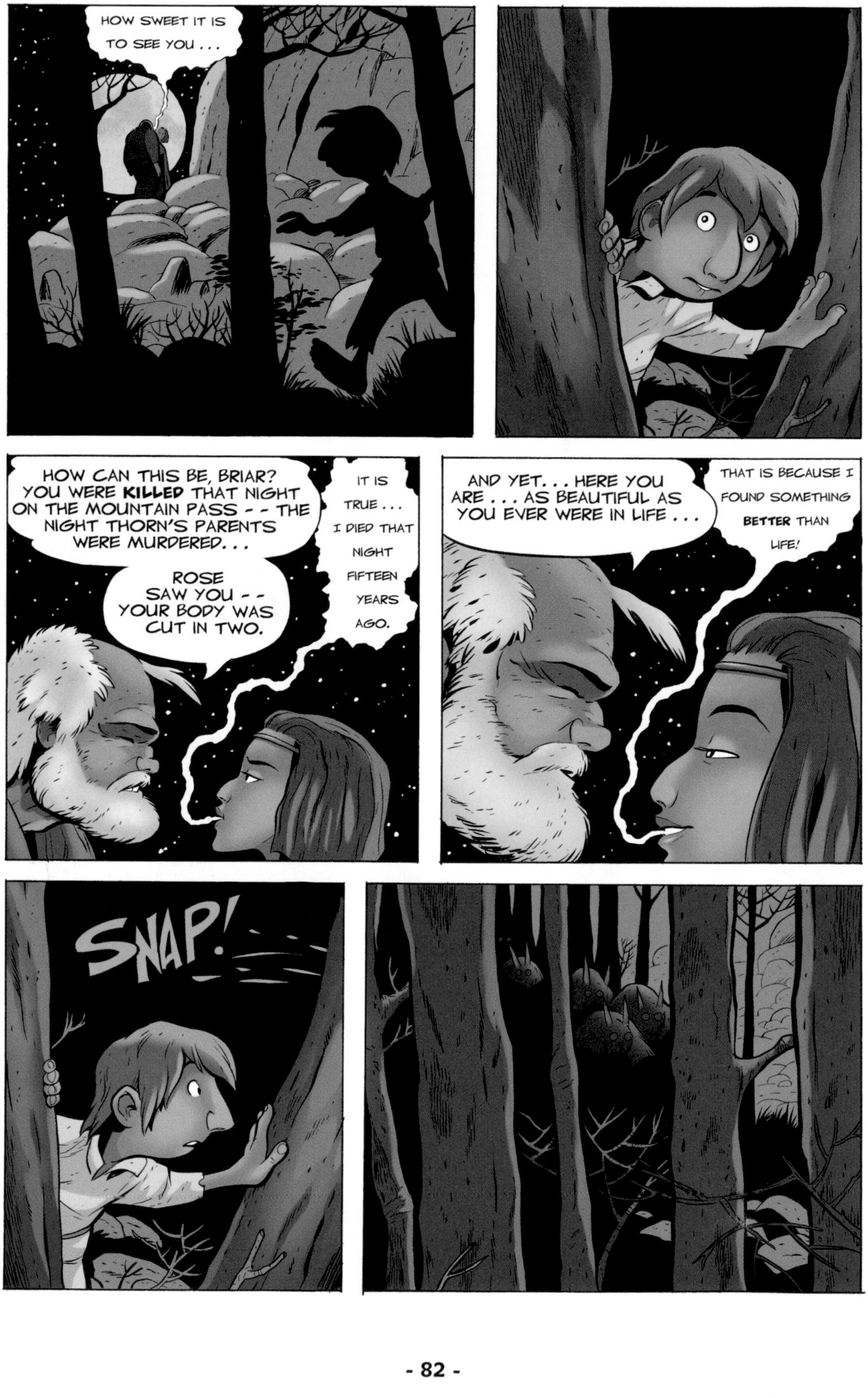
HOW SWEET IT IS TO SEE YOU . . .
HOW CAN THIS BE, BRIAR? YOU WERE KILLED THAT NIGHT ON THE MOUNTAIN PASS - - THE NIGHT THORN'S PARENTS WERE MURDERED . . .
ROSE SAW YOU - - YOUR BODY WAS CUT IN TWO.
IT IS TRUE . . . I DIED THAT NIGHT FIFTEEN YEARS AGO.
AND YET . . . HERE YOU ARE . . . AS BEAUTIFUL AS YOU EVER WERE IN LIFE . . .
THAT IS BECAUSE I FOUND SOMETHING BETTER THAN LIFE!
SNAP!

WHAT HAVE I DONE?

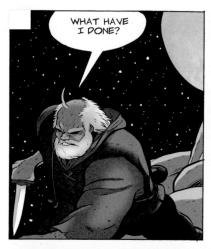

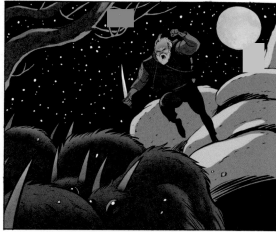

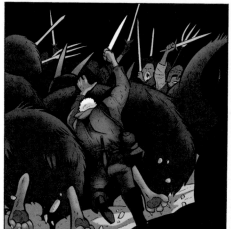

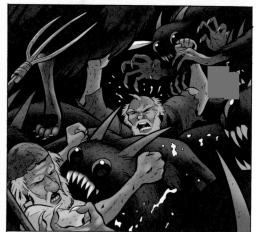

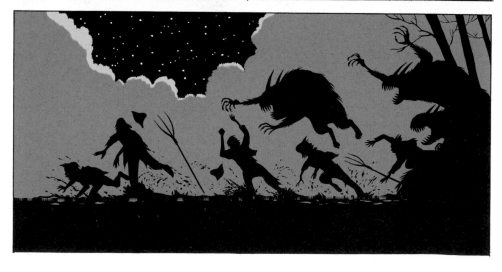

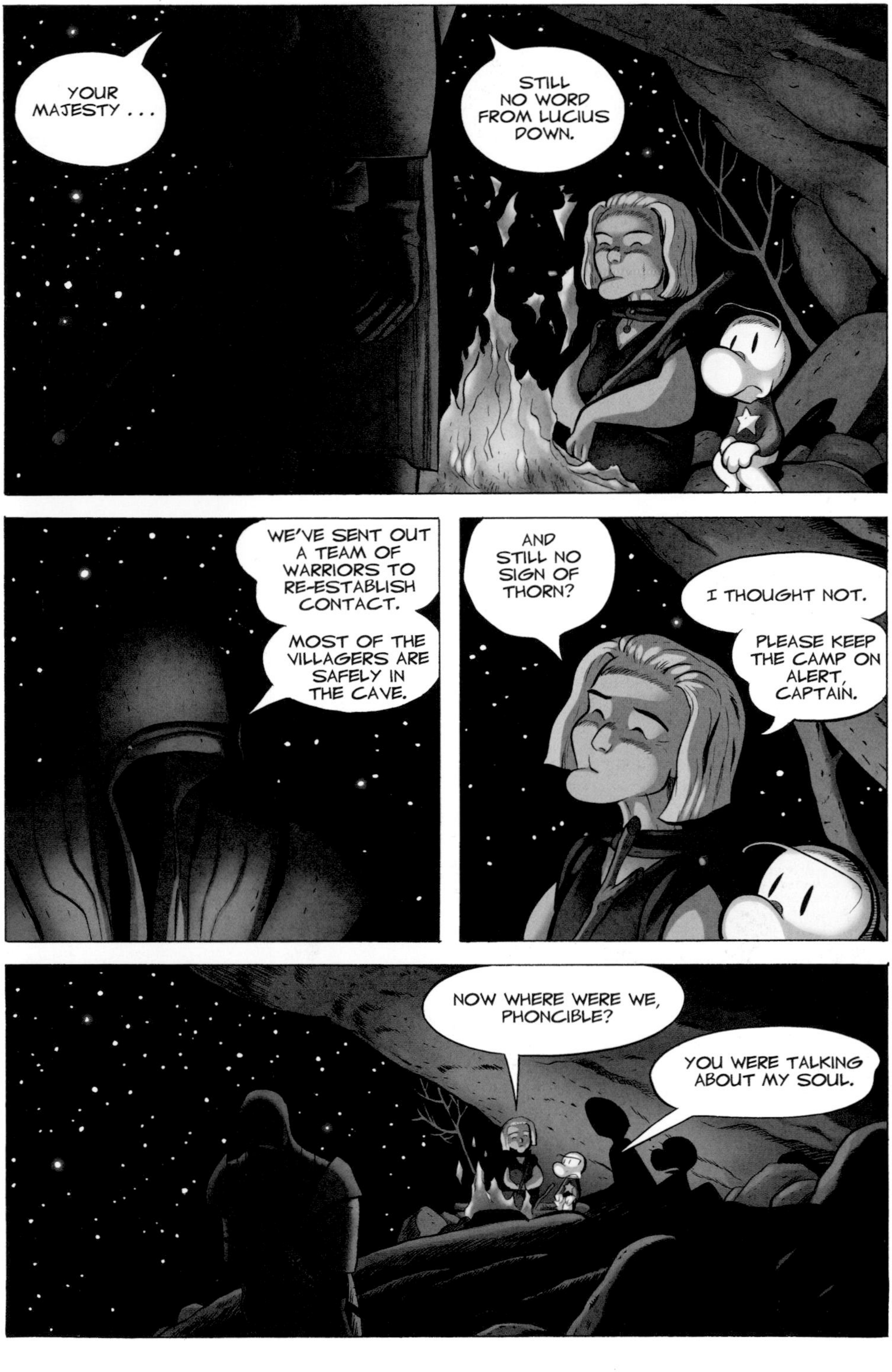
YOUR MAJESTY . . .
STILL NO WORD FROM LUCIUS DOWN.
WE'VE SENT OUT A TEAM OF WARRIORS TO RE-ESTABLISH CONTACT.
MOST OF THE VILLAGERS ARE SAFELY IN THE CAVE.
AND STILL NO SIGN OF THORN?
I THOUGHT NOT.
PLEASE KEEP THE CAMP ON ALERT, CAPTAIN.
NOW WHERE WERE WE, PHONCIBLE?
YOU WERE TALKING ABOUT MY SOUL.

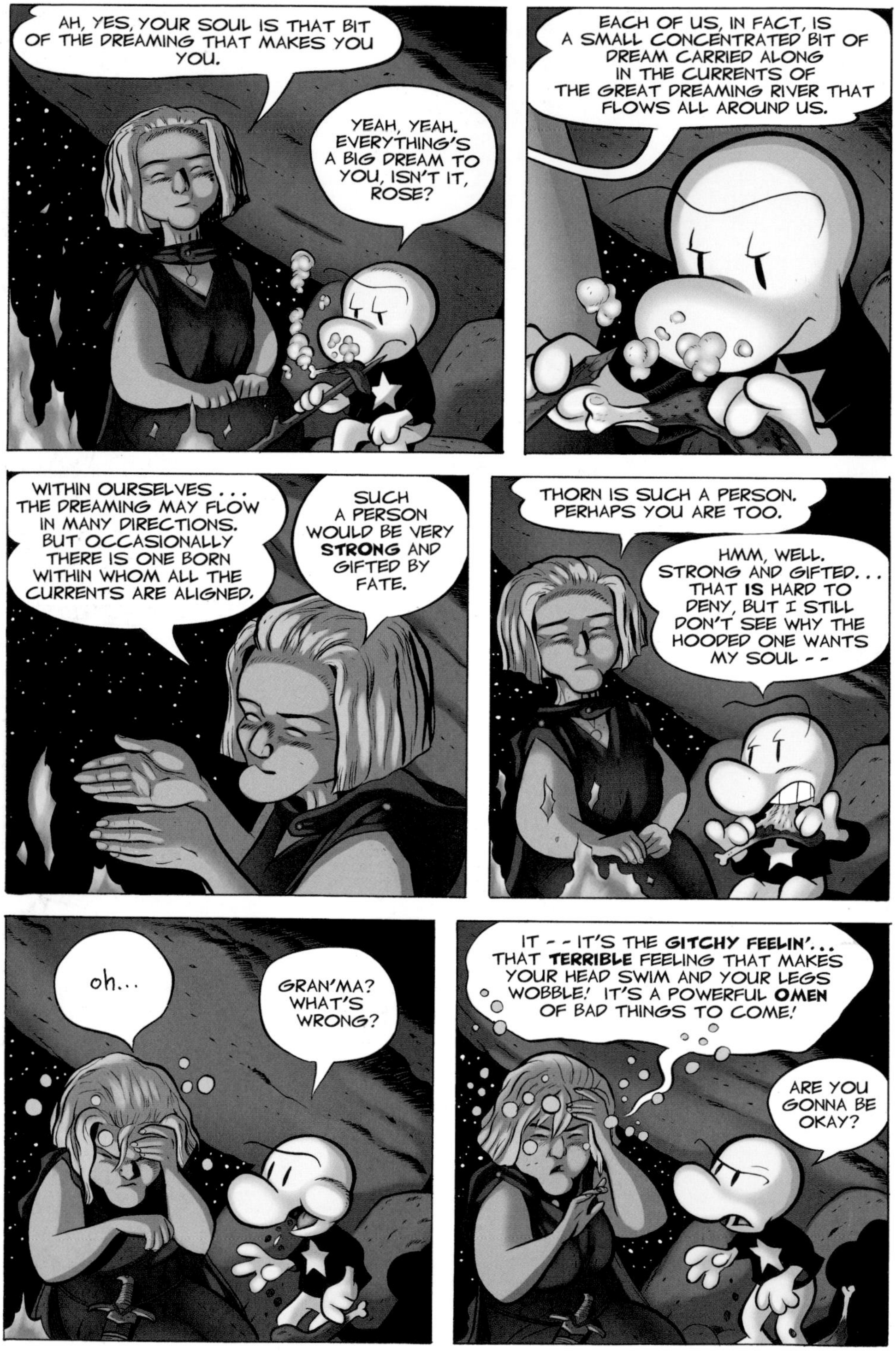
AH, YES, YOUR SOUL IS THAT BIT OF THE DREAMING THAT MAKES YOU YOU.
YEAH, YEAH. EVERYTHING'S A BIG DREAM TO YOU, ISN'T IT, ROSE?
EACH OF US, IN FACT, IS A SMALL CONCENTRATED BIT OF DREAM CARRIED ALONG IN THE CURRENTS OF THE GREAT DREAMING RIVER THAT FLOWS ALL AROUND US.
WITHIN OURSELVES . . . THE DREAMING MAY FLOW IN MANY DIRECTIONS. BUT OCCASIONALLY THERE IS ONE BORN WITHIN WHOM ALL THE CURRENTS ARE ALIGNED.
SUCH A PERSON WOULD BE VERY **STRONG** AND GIFTED BY FATE.
THORN IS SUCH A PERSON. PERHAPS YOU ARE TOO.
HMM, WELL. STRONG AND GIFTED. . . THAT **IS** HARD TO DENY, BUT I STILL DON'T SEE WHY THE HOODED ONE WANTS MY SOUL - -
oh...
GRAN'MA? WHAT'S WRONG?
IT - - IT'S THE **GITCHY FEELIN'**. . . THAT **TERRIBLE** FEELING THAT MAKES YOUR HEAD SWIM AND YOUR LEGS WOBBLE! IT'S A POWERFUL **OMEN** OF BAD THINGS TO COME!
ARE YOU GONNA BE OKAY?

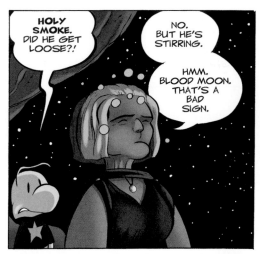

HOLY SMOKE. DID HE GET LOOSE?!

NO. BUT HE'S STIRRING.

HMM. BLOOD MOON. THAT'S A BAD SIGN.

YOUR HIGHNESS! LUCIUS IS OUTSIDE THE CAMP! HE AND HIS MEN ARE BEING PURSUED BY RAT CREATURES!

GET THEM INSIDE AND SECURE THE GATES.

LUCIUS! WHAT HAPPENED?

THE RATS CAUGHT US BY THE RIVER AND SLAUGHTERED US. IF REINFORCEMENTS HADN'T ARRIVED, WE WOULD'VE BEEN FINISHED.

I SHOULD HAVE BEEN WITH YOU.

I WISH YOU HAD BEEN . . . HERE. TAKE HIM. I DON'T KNOW IF HE'S STILL ALIVE OR NOT.

IT'S ALL MY FAULT, ROSE. THE RAT CREATURES HAVE US COMPLETELY SURROUNDED.

CALM. BE CALM. WE MUST PREPARE FOR OUR FINAL STAND.

I JUST PRAY THAT THORN IS SAFE . . . WHEREVER SHE IS.

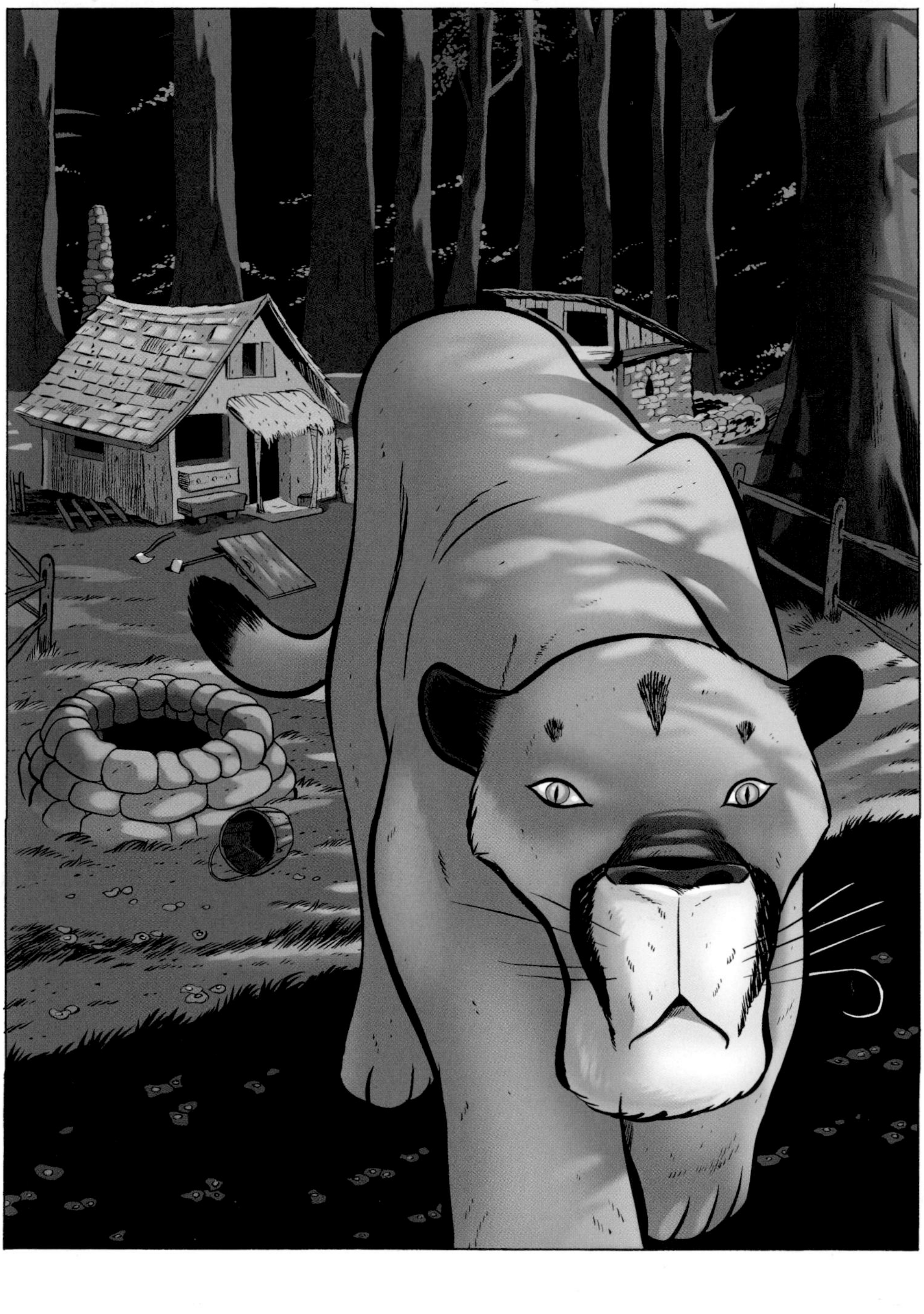

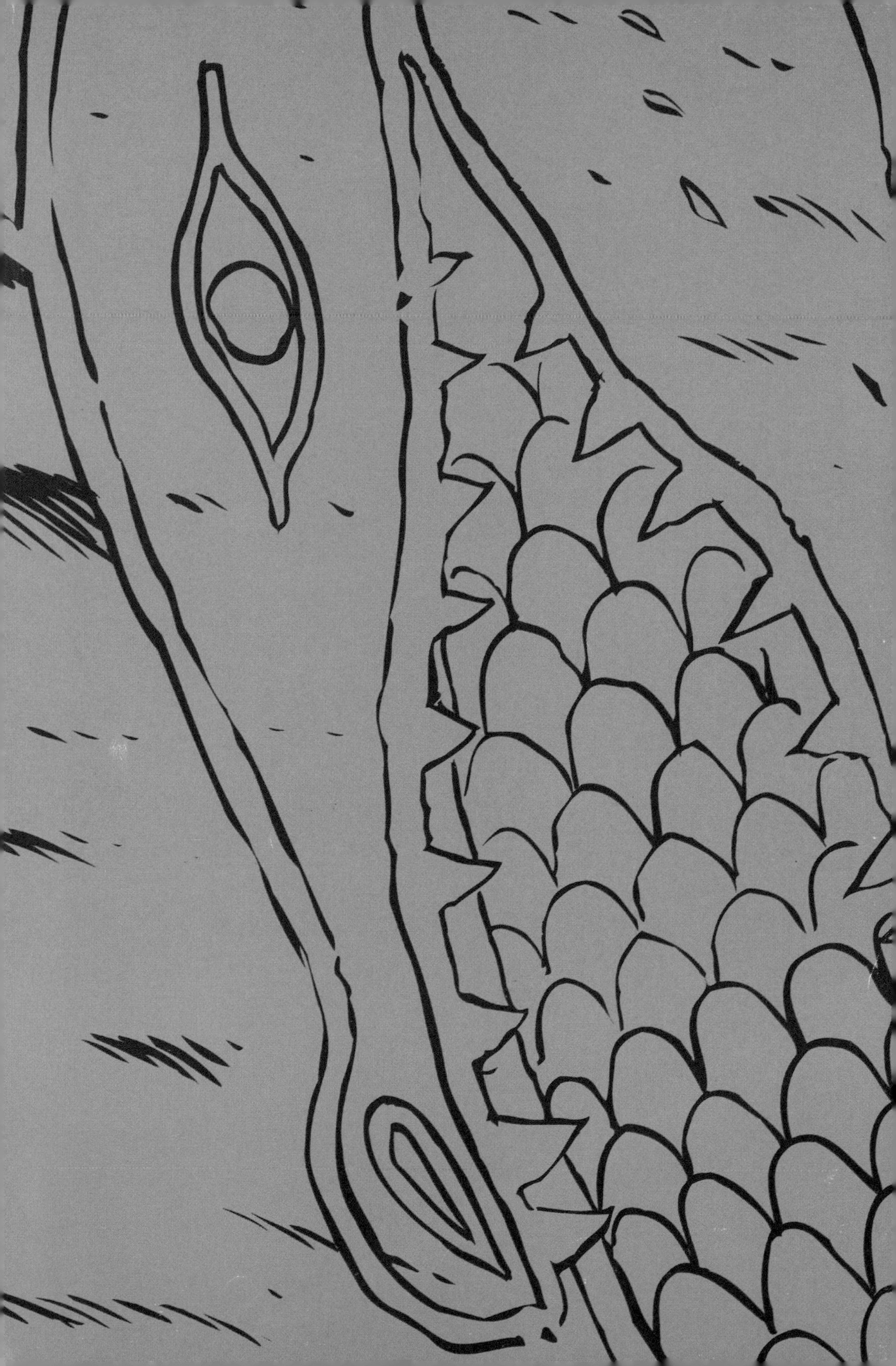

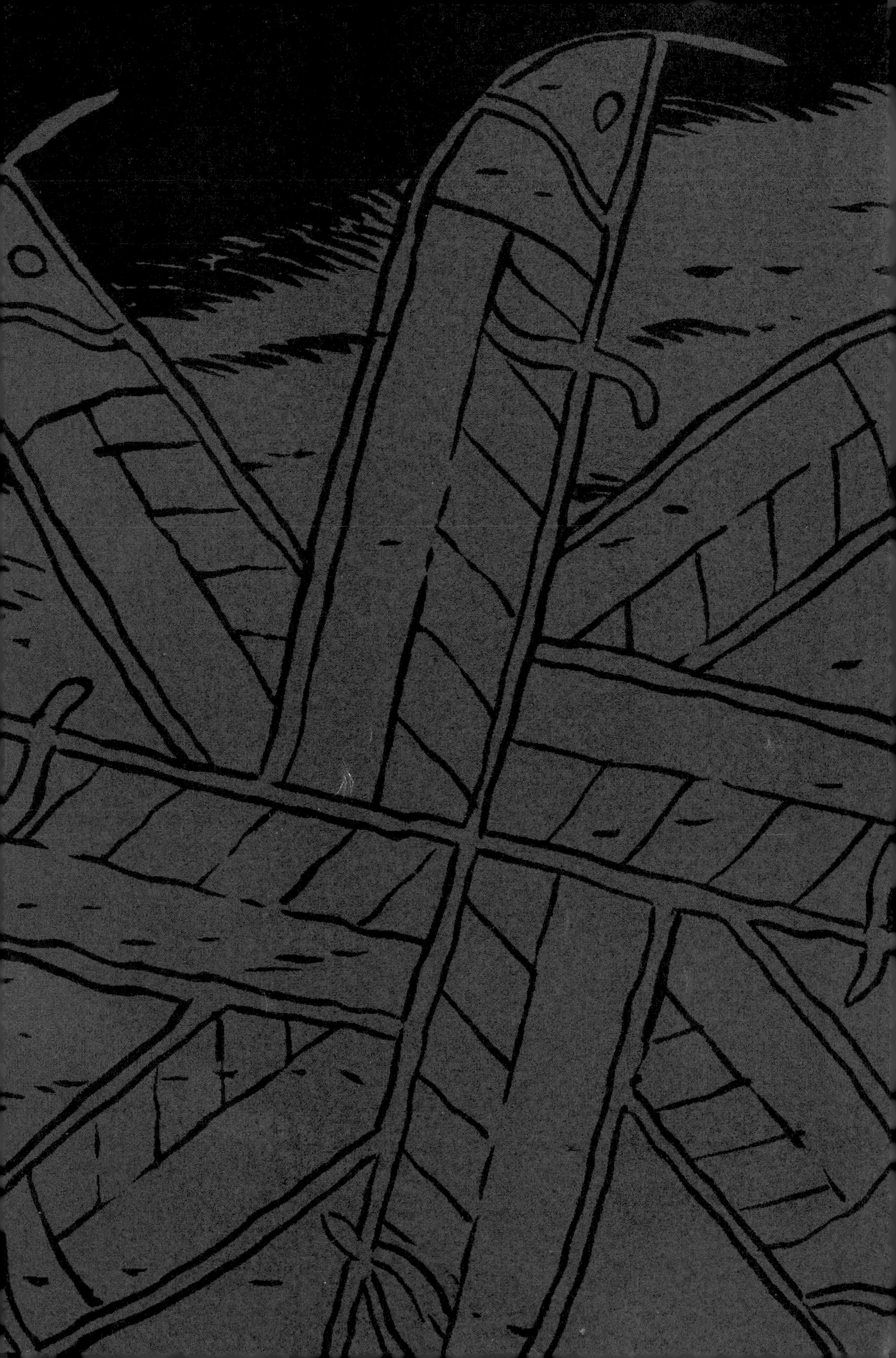

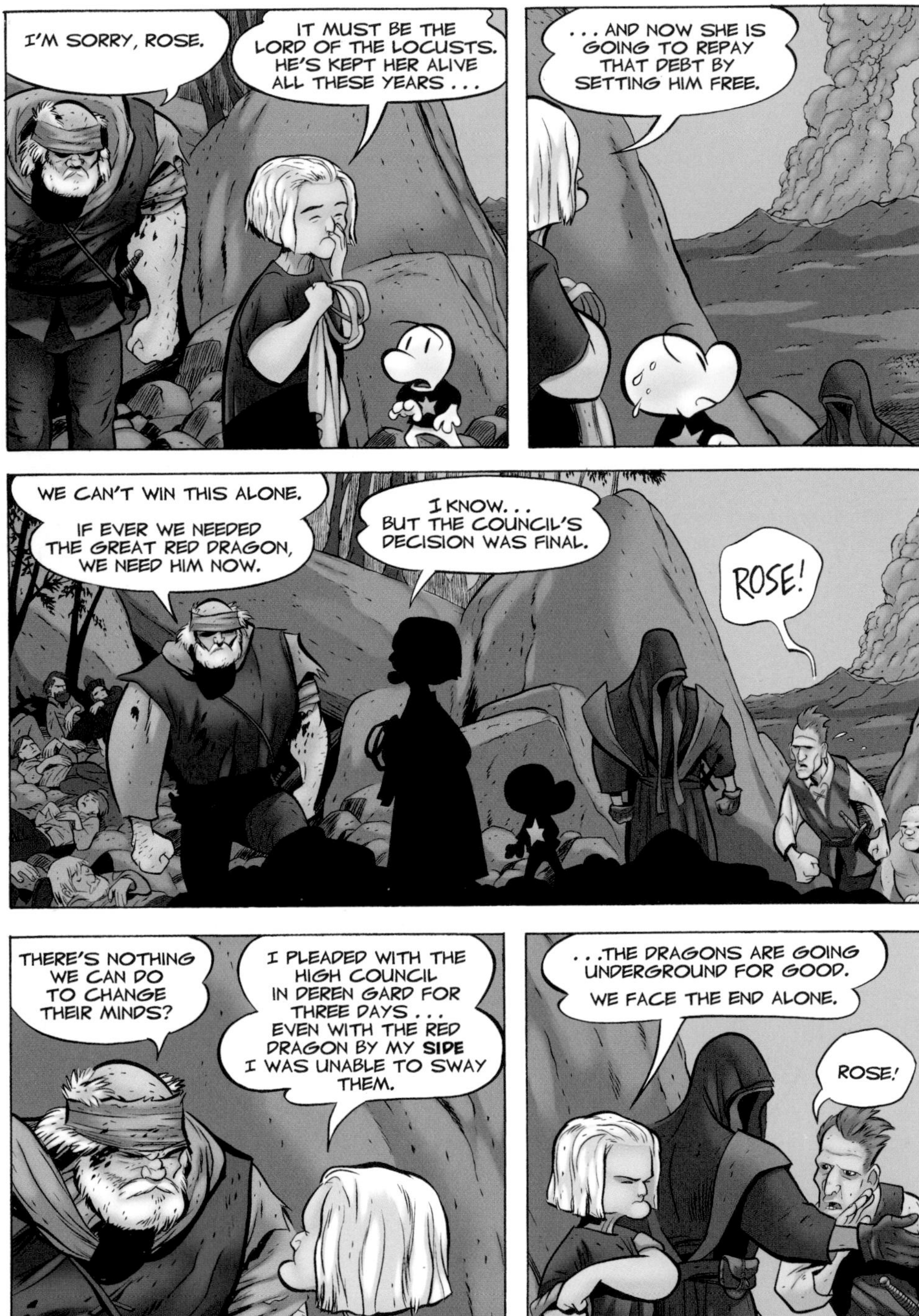
I'M SORRY, ROSE.
IT MUST BE THE LORD OF THE LOCUSTS. HE'S KEPT HER ALIVE ALL THESE YEARS . . .
. . . AND NOW SHE IS GOING TO REPAY THAT DEBT BY SETTING HIM FREE.
WE CAN'T WIN THIS ALONE.
IF EVER WE NEEDED THE GREAT RED DRAGON, WE NEED HIM NOW.
I KNOW. . . BUT THE COUNCIL'S DECISION WAS FINAL.
ROSE!
THERE'S NOTHING WE CAN DO TO CHANGE THEIR MINDS?
I PLEADED WITH THE HIGH COUNCIL IN DEREN GARD FOR THREE DAYS . . . EVEN WITH THE RED DRAGON BY MY SIDE I WAS UNABLE TO SWAY THEM.
. . .THE DRAGONS ARE GOING UNDERGROUND FOR GOOD.
WE FACE THE END ALONE.
ROSE!

IT'S ALL RIGHT, CAPTAIN. WHAT IS IT, WENDELL?

GIVE HIM TO US, ROSE!

YEAH! THIS IS ALL HIS FAULT!

WHOSE FAULT, DEAR?

PHONEY BONE! "THE ONE WHO BEARS THE STAR!"

HE'S THE ONE THE RAT CREATURES ARE AFTER. THEY TORE UP THE VALLEY LOOKING FOR HIM.

YEAH! NOW THE RAT CREATURES HAVE US SURROUNDED! IF HE'S ALL THEY WANT, LET'S HAND HIM OVER!

EVEN IF HE WAS ALL THE RAT CREATURES WANTED, I WOULDN'T ADVISE GIVING THEM THE ONE THING THEY NEED TO WIN THIS WAR.

WHAT DO YOU MEAN?

OUR FRIENDS OUT THERE BELIEVE THAT THE "ONE WHO BEARS THE STAR" CAN FREE THE ANCIENT LORD OF THE LOCUSTS.

LORD OF TH - -? YOU MEAN THAT OLD FABLE ABOUT THE QUEEN OF THE DRAGONS?

OH, FER- -

--THAT'S JUST A STORY! GIVE THEM PHONEY BONE AND LET 'EM TRY! WHAT CAN THE LORD OF THE LOCUSTS DO TO US?

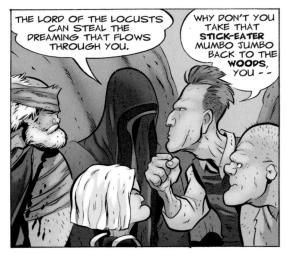

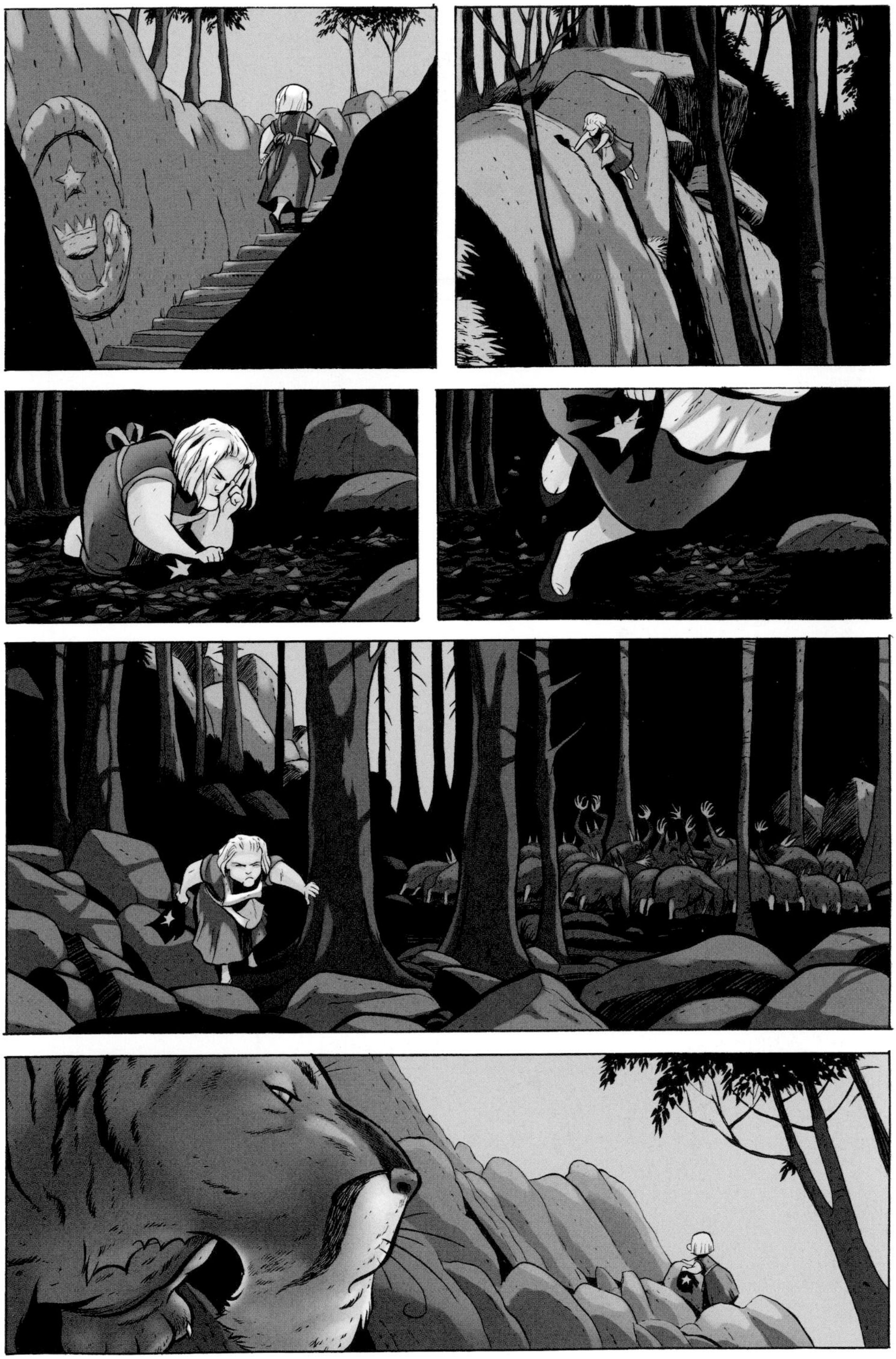

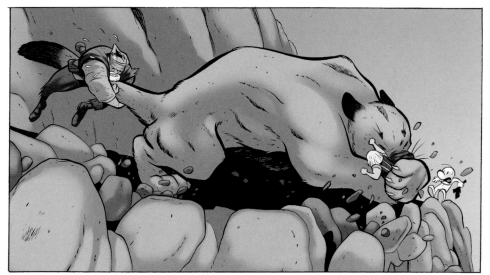

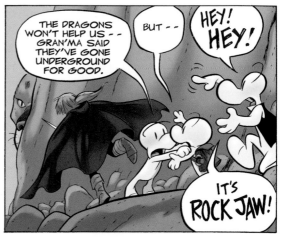

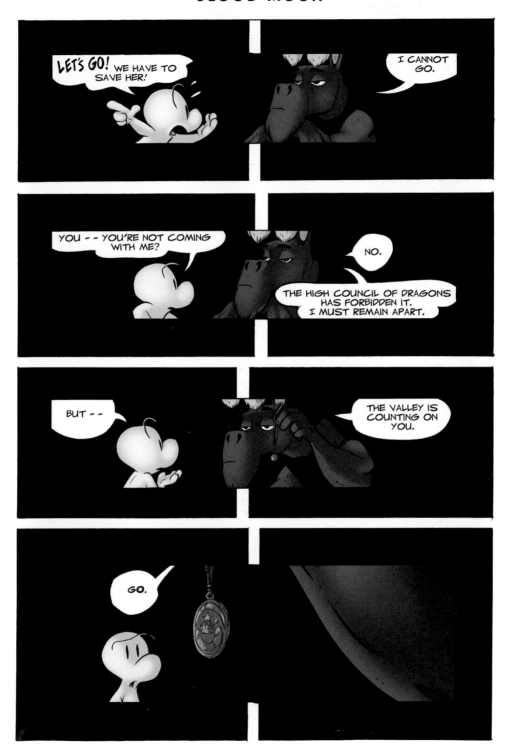

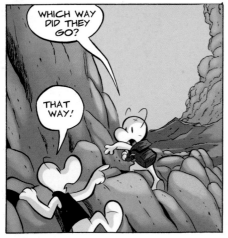

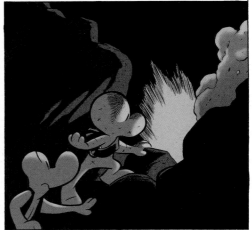

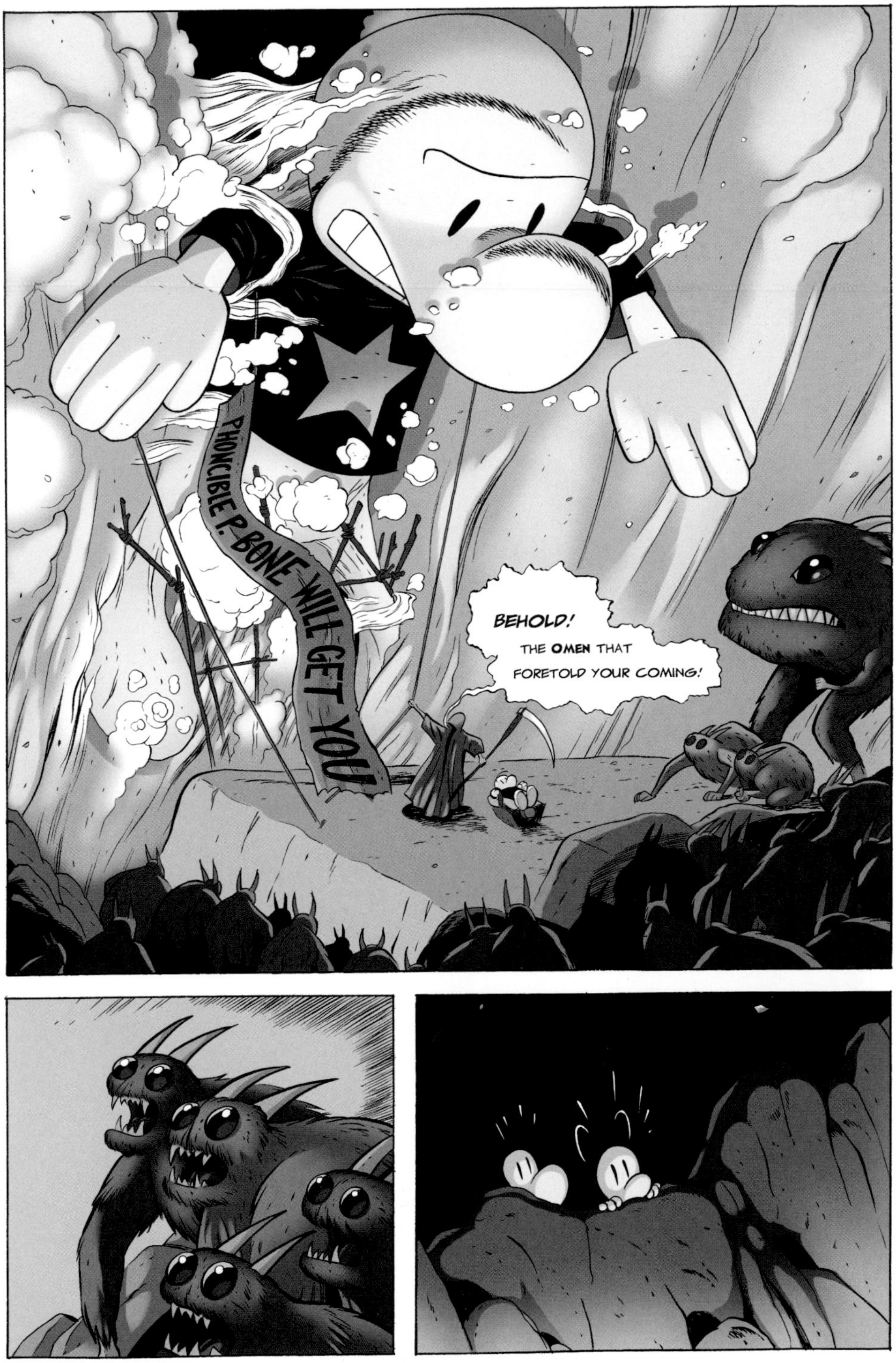
PHONCIBLE P. BONE WILL GET YOU
BEHOLD! THE OMEN THAT FORETOLD YOUR COMING!

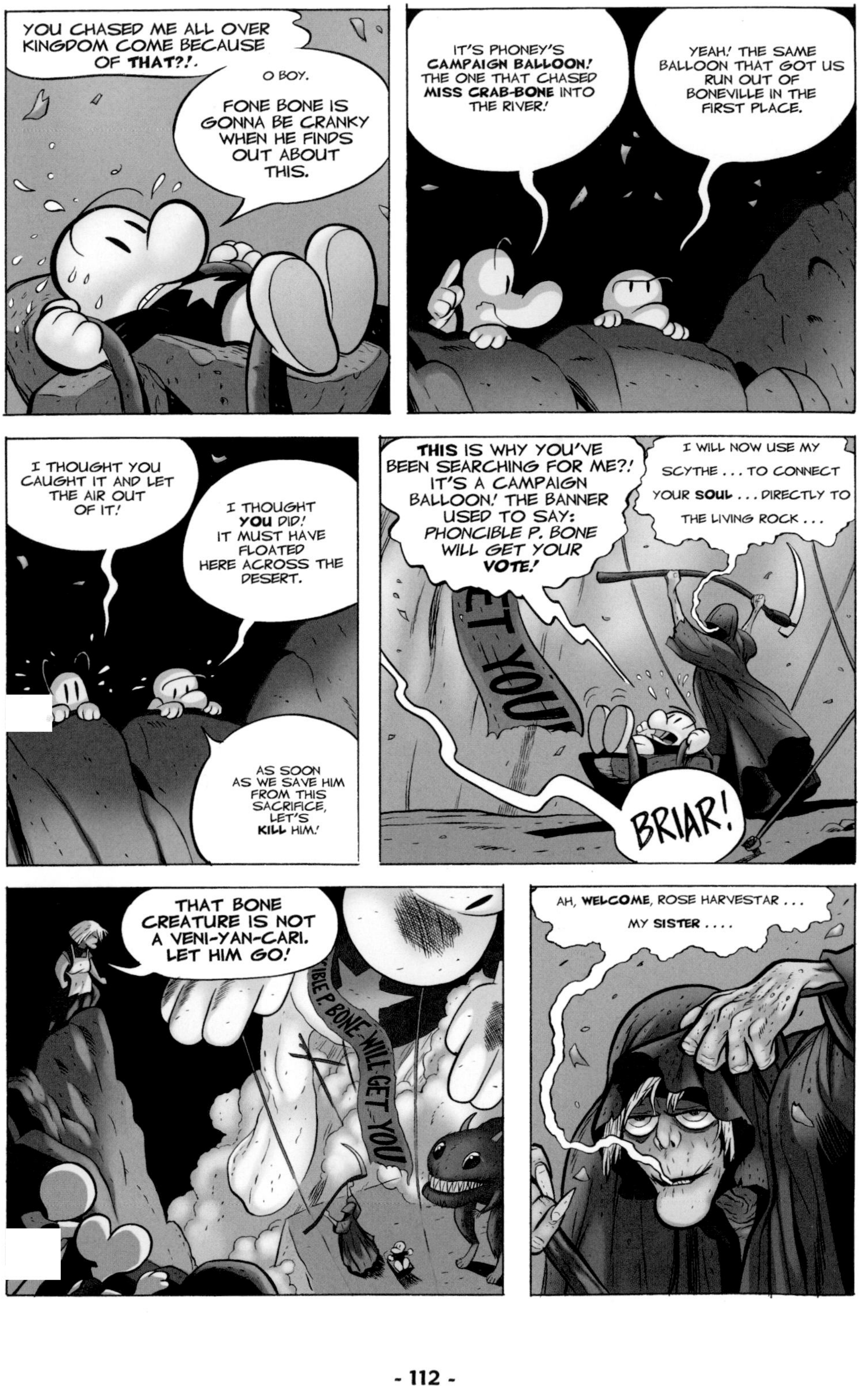
YOU CHASED ME ALL OVER KINGDOM COME BECAUSE OF **THAT**?!.
O BOY.
FONE BONE IS GONNA BE CRANKY WHEN HE FINDS OUT ABOUT THIS.
IT'S PHONEY'S **CAMPAIGN BALLOON!** THE ONE THAT CHASED **MISS CRAB-BONE** INTO THE RIVER!
YEAH! THE SAME BALLOON THAT GOT US RUN OUT OF BONEVILLE IN THE FIRST PLACE.
I THOUGHT YOU CAUGHT IT AND LET THE AIR OUT OF IT!
I THOUGHT **YOU** DID! IT MUST HAVE FLOATED HERE ACROSS THE DESERT.
AS SOON AS WE SAVE HIM FROM THIS SACRIFICE, LET'S **KILL** HIM!
THIS IS WHY YOU'VE BEEN SEARCHING FOR ME?! IT'S A CAMPAIGN BALLOON! THE BANNER USED TO SAY: *PHONCIBLE P. BONE WILL GET YOUR* **VOTE!**
I WILL NOW USE MY SCYTHE . . . TO CONNECT YOUR **SOUL** . . . DIRECTLY TO THE LIVING ROCK . . .
ET YOU
BRIAR!
THAT BONE CREATURE IS NOT A VENI-YAN-CARI. LET HIM GO!
CIBLE P. BONE WILL GET YOU
AH, **WELCOME**, ROSE HARVESTAR . . . MY **SISTER** . . . .

WHERE IS SHE, BRIAR?

I CONFESS, MY SISTER . . . THAT SEEING YOU ALIVE IS QUITE AMAZING . . .

. . . . I HAD THOUGHT YOU DIED THE SAME NIGHT I DID.

WHERE **IS** SHE, BRIAR?

HERE . . . IS YOUR PRECIOUS VENI-YAN-CARI . .

THE ONE **YOU** THOUGHT WOULD BE THE FUTURE RULER OF THE LAND. . .

. . . BUT SHE IS **DEAD!**

AS YOU BOTH **SHOULD** HAVE BEEN FIFTEEN YEARS AGO ON THAT MOUNTAIN PASS . . .

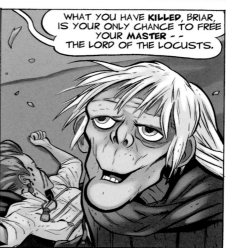

WHAT YOU HAVE **KILLED**, BRIAR, IS YOUR ONLY CHANCE TO FREE YOUR **MASTER** − − THE LORD OF THE LOCUSTS.

EVEN **I** CAN SEE THIS BALLOON IS NO OMEN OF **POWER** − − IT IS MERELY A SYMBOL OF **PRIDE** AND **VANITY!**

YOUR **JEALOUSY** OF THE TRUE VENI-YAN-CARI HAS BLINDED YOU − − AND YOU HAVE BADLY MISCALCULATED, MY **SISTER**.

NO . . .

NO, I HAVE NOT MISCALCULATED . . . HE **HAS** THE POWER TO FREE OUR MASTER -- HE **MUST!**

LISTEN, SIS . . . I ENJOY A HOSTILE TAKEOVER AS MUCH AS THE NEXT GUY, BUT FACE **FACTS!** YOU BLEW IT!

WHAT HAVE YOU **DONE,** STICK-EATER?

IT WAS THE **PRINCESS** WE NEEDED, NOT THE BONE! AND YOU HAD HER **KILLED!**

YOU HAVE BROUGHT DISGRACE UPON MY PEOPLE IN THE EYES OF THE LORD OF THE LOCUSTS . . .

WAIT -- DID YOU FEEL THAT?

SOMETHING MOVED DEEP IN THE EARTH!

FONE BONE! NO!

I'M GOING DOWN THERE!

THOOM

THOOM! hissss

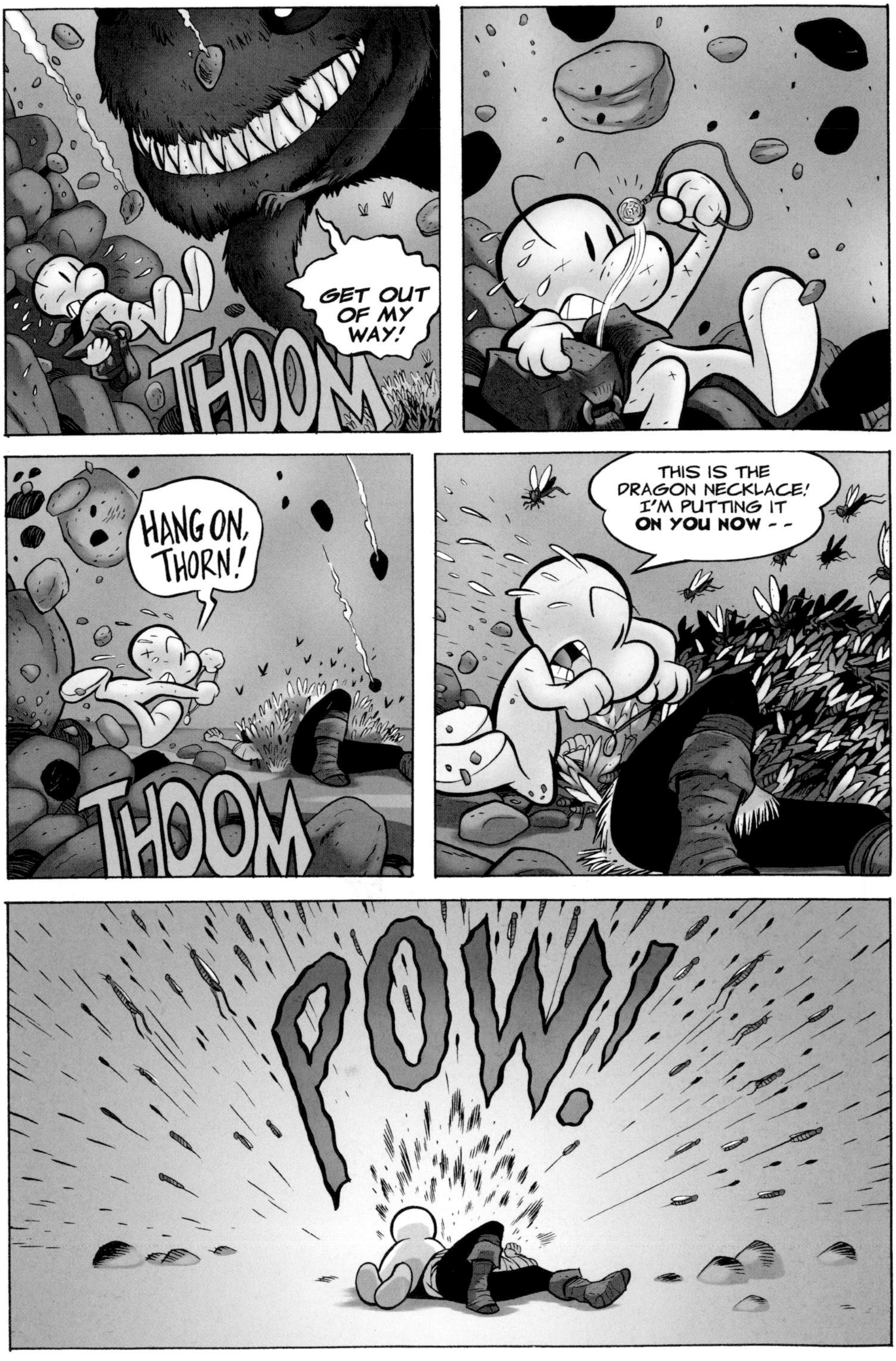
GET OUT OF MY WAY!
THOOM
HANG ON, THORN!
THOOM
THIS IS THE DRAGON NECKLACE! I'M PUTTING IT **ON YOU NOW - -**
POW!